Porter used to en̶......

But that was befo̶......

those same woods. Now he knew ......

evil. It hid violent forces, swift and terrible, forces that could take his life away. Instinct told him to turn around and run back to the light. To safety. To the Night Owl.

The Night Owl?

All of his troubles had begun in the Night Owl.

Maybe it was safer in the woods.

Except that it hadn't been safer for Booger.

Unless, like Tommy said, it had all been a practical joke for his benefit. To scare him. And if it had been a joke, it had certainly worked. Porter was definitely scared.

But Porter didn't think it was a joke. He stopped to get his bearings. It was stupid not to have brought a flashlight. Like so many other stupid things he had done lately. He found the trail he was looking for and walked to the spot where Booger had been murdered.

There was no corpse. Booger's body was gone.

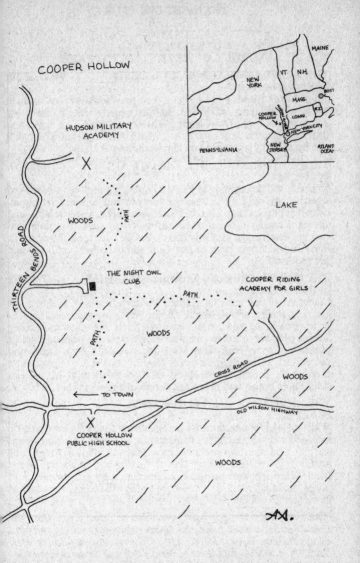

COOPER HOLLOW

HUDSON MILITARY
ACADEMY

X

WOODS

PATH

LAKE

THIRTEEN BENDS ROAD

THE NIGHT OWL
CLUB

PATH

COOPER RIDING
ACADEMY FOR GIRLS

X

PATH

WOODS

CROSS ROAD

WOODS

← TO TOWN

OLD WILSON HIGHWAY

X
COOPER HOLLOW
PUBLIC HIGH SCHOOL

WOODS

MAINE

NEW
YORK

VT. N.H.

MASS.

BOST

COOPER
HOLLOW

CONN.

R.I.

PENNSYLVANIA

NEW
JERSEY

NEW YORK CITY

ATLANTIC
OCEAN

THE NIGHT OWL CLUB
IT'S COOL—
IT'S FUN—
IT'S TERRIFYING—
AND YOU CAN JOIN IT . . . IF YOU DARE!

THE NIGHTMARE CLUB #1: JOY RIDE (4315, $3.50)
by Richard Lee Byers

All of Mike's friends know he has a problem—he doesn't see anything wrong with drinking and driving. But then a pretty new girl named Joy comes to The Night Owl Club, and she doesn't mind if he drinks and drives. In fact, she encourages it. And what Mike doesn't know might kill him because Joy is going to take him on the ride of his life!

THE NIGHTMARE CLUB #2: THE INITIATION (4316, $3.50)
by Nick Baron

Kimberly will do anything to join the hottest clique at her school. And when her boyfriend, Griff, objects to her new "bad" image, Kimberly decides that he is a wimp. Then kids start drowning in a nearby lake—and she starts having nightmares about an evil water spirit that has a hold over her new friends. Kimberly knows that she must resist the monster's horrible demands in order to save Griff and the other kids' lives—and her very soul!

THE NIGHTMARE CLUB #3: WARLOCK GAMES (4317, $3.50)
by Richard Lee Byers

Mark, the newest cadet at Hudson Military Academy, is falling for Laurie, a student at rival school, Cooper High. So, he does not want to be involved in the feud between the two schools. But fellow cadet, Greg Tobias, persuades Mark to join other cadets in playing weird and violent pranks on Cooper High. Then Mark discovers that Greg is a centuries-old warlock who is playing a deadly game of chess with a fellow demon in which the students are the pawns—and now Mark must break Greg's deadly hold or they will all become victims of a terrifying evil . . .

THE NIGHTMARE CLUB #4: THE MASK (4349, $3.50)
by Nick Baron

While looking for a costume for the Nightmare Club's Halloween party, average-looking Sheila finds a weird mask in a local antique barn. When she puts it on, she turns into a real knockout, and soon is getting lots of attention. Then good-looking kids start dying and Sheila realizes the truth. When she wears the mask, its guardian spirit gets stronger. And unless Sheila can resist its seductive magic she will become a prisoner of its murderous evil forever!

Available wherever paperbacks are sold, or order direct from the Publisher. Send cover price plus 50¢ per copy for mailing and handling to Zebra Books, Dept. 4450, 475 Park Avenue South, New York, N.Y. 10016. Residents of New York and Tennessee must include sales tax. DO NOT SEND CASH. For a free Zebra/Pinnacle catalog please write to the above address.

The Nightmare Club

#8: DEADLY STAKES

BRUCE RICHARDS

Z·FAVE
KENSINGTON PUBLISHING CORP.

Z-FAVE BOOKS are published by

Kensington Publishing Corp.
475 Park Avenue South
New York, NY 10016

First Printing: January, 1994

Printed in the United States of America

One

Porter Smith loved money. And he had learned at an early age how to make a lot of it. He started betting nickels with his dad when he was only seven. He almost never lost. Now, ten years later, he was taking bets from his classmates at the Hudson Military Academy and losing even less.

The groans from a crowd of cadets watching a basketball game on TV nearly drowned out the band's lead singer in the next room. Porter looked up from his slouch in the dark corner booth at the Night Owl Club and peered at the small black-and-white Motorola television perched above the bar. His light blue eyes were magnified behind his thick-lensed, wire-rimmed glasses.

Michael Jordan had scored again. Points fifty-one and fifty-two. The opposing coach quickly called a time out with a little under two minutes left in the game. Porter's eyes searched for the score before TNT rolled its commercials.

The Bulls would cover the spread, easily, he noticed. As he knew they would.

Most of the cadets watching the game—the ones who had groaned, at any rate—would owe him some money in about two minutes.

"Make me rich, Michael," Porter yelled in the direction of the bar.

He received glares in return, except from the plebes, who looked humbly down at their shoes. They could get fifty push-ups just for looking at a senior cadet—like Porter—the wrong way.

Porter was on scholarship to the prestigious Hudson Military Academy. He did well in most of his subjects, but he was a whiz when it came to numbers: percentages, odds, accounting. So, it was only natural for him to take sucker bets from his classmates, especially the fresh supply of gullible freshmen plebes who passed every semester through the sacred gates of the academy.

But it wasn't just his mastery of numbers that swung the odds in his favor. He had a *feel* for the game. Any game. A gift. A nearly infallible instinct. Even with the penny-ante bets he made with his classmates, he was still going to leave HMA with quite a little nest egg when he graduated.

Enough money to get him through Harvard or Stanford or one of the other elite colleges he had always dreamed of attending. All he had to do was keep his grades up and not do anything too stupid between now and graduation.

Like getting kicked out of the academy for being a bookie, for instance.

Which was why he was so discreet. Why he kept his operation small and quiet.

It was Friday night and the Night Owl was packed. Porter eyed a table of girls—probably from the Cooper Riding Academy, he figured. He watched them get up and amble toward the jukebox—the band was taking a break. The girls had that pampered look about them. Feeding quarters into the machine and punching buttons, their faces were illuminated by the light from the jukebox menu.

The jukebox kicked on and an Oldies number blared out.

One of the girls at the jukebox—cute, with long blond hair cascading from a velvet headband—let her gaze wander in Porter's direction.

Porter cocked his head to one side and gave the girl his most dazzling smile. Then he wiggled his ears. This rare talent had never actually gotten him a date, but at least it was good for a few laughs.

The cute blond giggled before turning away. She whispered something into the ear of the girl next to her, and the other girls turned toward Porter expectantly. Porter took his cue and renewed his ear wiggling. But the girls had better things to do than watch him wiggle his ears. They started to talk amongst themselves, occasionally looking in his direction.

Porter wasn't really interested in those girls, anyway. He had never had a girlfriend and probably wouldn't till he got out of this hick town with its preppy schools. Whenever thoughts of sex entered his mind—which was pretty often these days—he turned his attention to calculating the odds and collecting his winnings. He didn't have time for girls. His betting action was his excitement.

More groans from the bar. Jordan was somewhere above the rim jamming down another two. Porter was going to win big tonight.

The Night Owl was the favorite hangout for teenagers in Cooper Hollow. It was really the only spot where students from the different schools—HMA, Cooper Riding Academy, and Cooper Hollow High—actually mingled. Not that Porter did much mingling. Most nights he sat in his corner booth waiting for cadets to approach him with their bets, and later to come back to pay him what they lost.

Porter's gaze shifted from the girls back to the bar where some guys were joking and playfully punching each other as they watched the game. One of them turned and caught Porter's eye. "Good game, huh?" Porter said with a smile. But the cadet had already turned back to the game.

None of the other cadets even bothered to acknowledge Porter. He didn't mind. They could ignore him, so long as they paid what they owed. He was a businessman, a very successful businessman. No need to mix business with pleasure. He'd have plenty of time for that when he got to college. He knew girls liked a guy with money, and by the time he got to college, he'd have more than enough to lavish on the beautiful coeds. Being on scholarship at HMA meant he had to keep a low profile when it came to spending money. Sure, he had thousands in the bank, but he didn't want to have to answer any questions about how he came by that money. Questions that could lead him into big trouble and the end of his gambling operation.

Jordan dunked another ball in the face of the opposing team's center, a rookie phenom, the number one draft pick in professional basketball. It was near the end of the game, the point in the contest where Jordan usually chose to do his worst damage, and the rookie was being taught a quick and savage lesson by the game's greatest player.

The phenom was the projected savior of his team, and his team was hot coming into this game with the Bulls. They were riding the crest of a six game winning streak and were an easy favorite to beat the Bulls in Chicago.

A sucker bet, Porter knew, and would collect heavily because of it.

Statistics were helpful, but sometimes you had to look beyond the numbers and into the heads of the athletes involved. That's where you found the edge. This was the *first* game *ever* between Jordan and the phenom. The *Savior* had been getting heavy press but Air Jordan was still the *Master.*

And he would want to prove it on national TV.

That was the essence of Michael Jordan, the greatest player to ever play the game, Porter knew. His ego was as great as his talent.

Michael popped in a three pointer from downtown.

And he knew how to beat the odds.

"Beautiful!" Porter shouted. And jumped up from his seat.

The girls at the jukebox looked over at him in disgust as if he had just farted loudly.

Porter self-consciously ran his fingers through his

thick, unruly brown hair which was cut short, cadet style. He smiled sheepishly at the girls and sat down.

The game was now definitely out of reach. From his shirt pocket, Porter withdrew a little black book—by far his most precious possession.

The book was written in an elaborate numerical code. It had the dates of all the games he covered; the spread; the final scores; and the biggest column of all, a list of all the cadets who owed him money.

Porter uncapped a black felt pen and began putting check marks next to most of the names.

The flickering yellow flame of the table's candle cast shadows on the pages of his black book, obscuring, then highlighting the names of his wealthy classmates.

Porter loved extracting the monthly allowances from the stuck-up types that made up a large percentage of the cadets who attended the Hudson Military Academy.

So polished and privileged and stiff. So full of themselves. Porter occasionally felt pangs of jealousy, especially when he saw them with pretty girls—girls who wouldn't look twice at Porter. But his contempt for them overshadowed his envy, and Porter convinced himself that most of his classmates were nothing more than worthless jerks. He wouldn't want to be friends with them even if they did condescend to include him in their ranks. And the girls that went out with them got what they wanted—a free meal and some rough sex.

Porter was accustomed to being a loner. From the first grade on, he had been a math nerd and was teased unmercifully by the same kinds of guys who ended up at HMA. So now every penny Porter took from them was sweet revenge.

And one step closer to college and away from the stifling atmosphere of the academy.

He wouldn't even be at the academy if it wasn't for his father, a decorated Vietnam War veteran turned drunk. The old man had encouraged him to apply for a scholarship to HMA. Badgered him, really. His father felt a military school was just what was needed to toughen Porter up and make a man of him.

His father had never come out and said it, but Porter knew his father thought he was weak—a sissy. Porter was no macho man, but he wasn't weak, either. Not weak like he knew his father was—slowly drinking himself to death. He finally succeeded one night during Porter's freshman year at the academy— a heart attack in the toilet of the local bar.

But not before he had extracted a promise from Porter the night before to graduate from the academy. A promise that Porter couldn't take back now.

Porter didn't take his promises too seriously anymore.

Still, Porter had loved and respected his father, although why he didn't know.

After his father died, Porter's mother took a part-time job at Reeves Textiles, a mill on the outskirts of Cooper Hollow. It was a nothing job, sitting in front of a computer all day punching in numbers, when she wasn't being chased around it by the mill owner, a total jerk named Reginald Reeves III. He was the father of a classmate of Porter's at the academy—Reginald IV—also a total jerk.

Porter wished he could tell her that he was making at least *three* times as much money as she was with his gambling operation. In a good month. More than enough to pay for both their needs and then some. But she wouldn't understand. Porter couldn't risk it, so he kept it to himself.

Porter nodded as Reginald Reeves IV, with his slicked back moussed hair, slid into the booth next to him.

Reggie was smaller than Porter by a couple of inches, but muscular, and possessed the aristocratic good looks that the snotty girls who attended the Cooper Riding Academy seemed to fall for. He was also smug beyond endurance, but Porter tolerated him because he was a good customer—Reggie usually lost a lot of money to him.

"Looks like you lucked out again, Smith," Reggie said, pulling several crisp, new bills from his soft leather wallet and stuffing them into the pocket of Porter's flannel shirt as if he were tipping a bellboy at a posh hotel.

"I don't need luck to beat *you,* Reggie," Porter said. Reggie's arrogance was typical of the blue bloods at the academy, but his money was still green. Porter removed the wad of bills from his pocket and counted them before making a mark next to Reggie's name.

"What's the matter, chief? Think I'd cheat you?"

"I *know* you'd cheat me, Reggie. You've done it before. Especially since you have so much trouble counting past ten when you run out of fingers."

Reggie's smug smile vanished. He looked at Porter as if inspecting a new species of insect. "I don't have

14

to know how to count, that's why my family hires peons like your mother."

Porter felt his face grow hot with anger and embarrassment. He was tempted to tell Reggie where he could stuff his money. But it was hard to tell a guy to stuff it when he was sending money your way every week hand over fist. "You know Reggie, I really feel sorry for you—"

"You feel sorry for *me?"*

"Yeah. You're looking a little tired. Worn out. I guess it's from reaching into your pocket so often to hand over all that allowance money your rich daddy gives you every week. So I'm going to do you a favor. I'm actually going to give you a chance to earn some of it back. You want the Knicks over the Lakers?"

"Where are they playing?" Reggie asked suspiciously.

"In the Garden." Porter answered. Madison Square Garden was the Knicks' home court, where they almost never lost a game.

"What's the spot?"

"The official line is nine. I'll give you the Knicks and . . . seven—make it six."

"Six . . ." Reggie mulled it over. "How about raising the ante a little?"

Porter didn't normally take bets over twenty dollars. But for a loser like Reggie, he would gladly make an exception. "A hundred?"

"Two hundred."

Porter shrugged. "Okay, two hundred."

"All right!" Reggie said eagerly as if he expected Porter to change his mind. Then he hesitated. "Hey

. . . Magic Johnson didn't come out of retirement, did he?"

"Nope." Porter said, jotting the bet down in his little black book.

Reggie slid out of the booth with a big, confident grin on his face. "I'll pick up my winnings Sunday night. You can always find me over in the billiards room if you ever come up with the balls to play me a game."

"Okay. *Chief,*" Porter said. Patronizing bastard. Porter had no intention of playing pool with Reggie. If there was one thing Reggie could do well, Porter knew, it was shoot pool. Reggie might suck as a gambler, but he could make a cue ball sit up and bark. Porter suspected that Reggie made back most of the money he lost to him at the pool table.

Porter scanned the crowd at the Night Owl Club and wondered which of his other suckers would be making his way to the booth next.

This was the best part. The payoff. The part where he rubbed it in a little to some of the uppity cadets. It was a good strategic move. As long as he didn't get his butt kicked. It was one of the reasons the suckers kept coming back for more. Suckers like Reggie Reeves. They couldn't let a skinny math nerd like Porter Smith whip them. They didn't believe Porter could keep beating them, month after month, year after year. The odds had to eventually even out in *their* favor. Didn't they? After all, the world owed them everything—their looks, their money, their exalted place in society. No way could Porter Smith—a little peon creep from the wrong side of the tracks—keep beating *them.*

Porter knew that so long as they thought like that, he'd keep winning, and winning big.

The loathing he felt for them cut into him like a jagged knife. He'd show them all. Every last damn one of them. He'd make more money than all of them put together.

Porter lost his train of thought. Had he forgotten something important? he wondered. He looked through the smoky, dimly lit room, at the shifting motion of bodies that now seemed oddly out of rhythm. Then he felt it again—a strange, overwhelming sensation in his mind. It was like his brain was being tugged by an invisible, psychic thread.

His eyes came to rest on Jenny Demos, who was staring at him from behind the bar.

Even in the murky haze of the club, Porter noticed the strange light of her violet-blue eyes. He felt entranced, stuck in time. It was as if everyone around him were moving in a dream, except for Jenny, boring into him with those flawlessly clear, bright eyes.

Porter averted his gaze and forced his eyes shut.

The tugging slowly subsided.

Jesus, Porter thought, shaking his head, what the hell was that? He took his glasses off and carefully wiped the lenses with the tail of his shirt. Maybe he needed a new prescription or something.

Jenny worked at the club helping out her father, Jake Demos, who ran the Night Owl Club. Porter thought Jenny was one of the prettiest women he had ever known, with her violet eyes and ash-blond hair. He fantasized about her all the time, even though she was a little old for him. He figured she was at least twenty.

Porter was first attracted to Jenny on account of her bright, mysterious violet-blue eyes. The type of eyes that had depth to them. The type of eyes that held secrets. The type of eyes that could, apparently, tug at a guy's brains.

So why had she turned those beautiful eyes on him?

She was looking at him again.

Porter looked the other way, at Reggie, who was standing by the jukebox with the girls Porter had noticed earlier. They were giving Reggie more attention in that moment than Porter could expect from them in a lifetime. Porter shook his head—girls are so predictable, he thought. Reggie's probably already impressed them with xeroxed copies of his family's bank account.

Time to call it a night, Porter decided.

He put his little black book away and grabbed his denim jacket. Usually Porter stuck around the Night Owl later on Friday nights to collect more money. But the basketball team was upstate for a big game, and a lot of the cadets had followed the team to cheer them on.

Porter slid out of his booth and walked across the floor purposefully avoiding looking in Jenny's direction. He couldn't get over the feeling that she had done something to him. Something weird.

Porter walked out of the club into the cool night air. He stared into the darkness of the parking lot, wishing for the millionth time that Jake would put some lights up so he could find his damn car a little more easily.

His eyes slowly adjusted to the night and he saw

his car—a big, beat-up dingy gray 1983 Oldsmobile. It was always the biggest car in the lot and easy to spot with its rear end sticking way out. It was an old car, and it didn't look like much, but it was big and spacious and solidly built with a massive engine that purred like a newborn kitten. The big tank-like car gave Porter a sense of security. Especially since he was such a lousy driver.

Porter walked toward his car feeling pretty smug— he had won several hundred dollars on tonight's game. He was halfway across the lot when he was blinded by a bright light. He turned toward the source and was spotlighted by the glaring headlights of an onrushing car.

Porter's jaw dropped, and he felt a rush of air leave his body. He wanted to run, but he was frozen in that spot like a petrified animal as the car came roaring right at him!

Two

With an ear-splitting screech, the car braked just inches in front of Porter. Porter felt his knees buckle, and he leaned against the side of the car—a beat-up black '64 Thunderbird—for support.

"Are you crazy?" Porter yelled in the direction of the driver. "You could have killed me, you imbecile!" Now that he knew he wasn't going to get run over, Porter felt a rush of rage that gave him renewed strength. He banged on the side of the car for emphasis. "Don't drink and drive, asshole," he continued, figuring some Cooper Hollow High students were joy riding with a six pack, as many around there were known to do on a regular basis.

Just as Porter was about to hurl some more insults, the passenger-side door flung open and a large guy with a flame of frizzy red hair bounced out and grabbed Porter by his flannel shirt, practically picking him up off the ground.

"Whoa!" Porter yelped, immediately regretting losing his temper. "Time out, dude!"

But the man didn't pay any attention to what Porter

was saying. He just tossed Porter into the front seat, next to the driver and climbed in after him. Porter's head banged into the steering wheel, and he heard the front door slam shut. The driver popped the clutch and the car shot forward throwing Porter back against the seat.

Then the Thunderbird blasted out of the parking lot.

Porter was used to getting out of tough situations—it was part of the game he played. But the guys he dealt with were cadets like himself, not big burly thugs who played rough. He rubbed the side of his head where he had banged the steering wheel.

"Ah, fellas . . ." Porter said as he sat up. He had to shout over the loud rock music blaring through the car speakers. "Uh, I don't remember calling for a cab."

Porter heard a little snicker from the back seat.

"You're a funny guy," said the driver. Except he wasn't laughing. "Isn't he a funny guy, Booger?"

"Yeah," a kid in the backseat mumbled.

Porter studied the driver hunched over the wheel. He was a pale, mean-looking young man with pinkish eyes and spiky bleached blond hair. He wore a full length black leather jacket over jeans and motorcycle boots. His right ear was pierced with a tiny black and white earring in the shape of a pair of tiny dice. They matched the two big fuzzy ones that hung down from the rearview mirror.

The guy was obviously into dice.

The driver reached down between his legs and grabbed a long neck bottle of beer, took a swig, and turned toward Porter. He glared at Porter, then belched in his face with breath that smelled like stale beer and dead meat.

"I guess I should introduce myself. My name's Skip Jagger," the driver said, yanking back on the steering wheel as the car nearly veered off the road. "That big handsome fellow sitting next to you is my brother, Red. And the squirt in the backseat is Booger."

"Burger," Booger corrected Skip. "Freddy Burger."

Porter glanced nervously over his shoulder at a skinny kid with a smattering of pimples. He wore a red and white Cooper Hollow High Red Devils school jacket. Long, greasy black hair jutted out from beneath a Red Devils cap. He guessed the kid was probably about fifteen. The other two were older—in their early twenties.

"We wanted to introduce ourselves," Skip drawled. "Since we're going to be business partners."

"Glad to meet ya," Porter shouted over the blaring rock music. Porter realized that even if he wanted to try to jump from the moving car, there was no way to get around Big Red, who was looking over his shoulder into the back of the car.

When Red noticed Porter eyeing the door, he slipped a large red, hairy arm around Porter's neck. "Don't even think about it, twerp," Red warned, slowly applying pressure to his jugular. "Or I'll pop your eyes out of your head like raw eggs."

"I've been watching you for over two weeks now," Skip said, dividing his attention between Porter and Thirteen Bends Road, which Porter knew really required a driver's undivided attention, especially when balancing a beer between your legs. "I've seen you sitting in your little corner booth just as happy as can be collecting your money every night. I said, 'Red, I smell us a business opportunity' didn't I, Red?"

"You sure did," Red said, releasing Porter's neck and running a fat thumb over his collar bone. Porter gasped for air.

"I really don't know what you guys are talking—" Porter felt a sudden shock of white pain as Red pressed down on his collar bone. Then he felt his little black book yanked out of his shirt pocket.

"What do we have here? Love letters?" Red asked, flicking through Porter's little black book with a baffled expression on his face. "Hey Booger, maybe you should take a look at this?" Red carelessly flipped Porter's black book over his shoulder before giving him a moronic grin. "Booger's good at numbers." The car hit a pothole and nearly swerved off the road. Skip jerked the wheel to get the car back on course.

Porter gripped the front edge of the seat and watched two long lines of trees on either side of the road fly past them like graphics in a video game. Porter wondered if he would ever get out of this car in one piece. There were a lot of car accidents on this road, and most of them were fatal.

Skip glanced over his shoulder at Booger. "See anything interesting in that book, Booger?"

"A lot of action, but he's light on the green side," Booger said.

Porter heard a click.

"I figured he might be." Skip said, finishing the beer with one long swallow and tossing the empty bottle out the open window. They were going too fast for Porter to hear it crash. Skip looked over at Porter with disdain. "Nothing but a damn lightweight. Well, we'll have to do something about that I guess—" Skip turned back to the road and hit the brakes just in time to avoid hitting a slow moving truck in front of them.

Porter slammed forward, hitting the radio and inadvertently changing the station. The sweet gentle harmonies of the Beach Boys came wafting through the loudspeakers. Skip downshifted, floored the T-Bird and shot around the truck.

Red yanked Porter back up into the seat. "Hey boy! You don't like my music?" Red poked a different button and the rock came blaring back into the car. It was a Pearl Jam number Porter recognized.

"Have you had enough time to think about our little proposition or what?" Skip asked impatiently, looking over at Porter as he shifted through the gears.

"What proposition—"

Skip hit a bump in the road and the car went airborne. Porter gripped the edge of the seat so tightly he left marks in the plastic vinyl.

The car hit the road again, bottoming out the shocks, as Skip fought the wheel. Porter was ready to agree to anything—just to get out of the car—if he only knew what the hell they wanted. "Cat's got his tongue, Skip. But I know some ways to loosen it!" Red shouted over the music.

Porter watched a rabbit hop out onto the road, and then freeze in the glare of car's headlights. Skip swerved *to hit the rabbit*. The black Thunderbird screamed down on the rabbit and hit it head on, smashing it flat. Its body burst open like a paper bag full of raw hamburger. The rabbit flipped into the air, mashing into the windshield with a red smear, before disappearing into the night.

"Nice shot, Skip," Red chortled.

"I guess we'll have to run her through the car wash again." Skip was laughing hysterically. Porter was mesmerized by the smear of rabbit gore and entrails still stuck to the windshield. It was what he imagined his face would look like after it went through the windshield. Porter felt behind his back for the seat belt but came up empty.

Meanwhile, Red had joined in the maniacal laughter.

"All right, pinhead, this is the deal!" Skip bellowed over the music. "We'll back you financially so you can raise the ante on your bets. That way we'll all make money. No need to be greedy, is there?" Skip asked Porter, looking over at him. "It ain't right you hogging all the action for yourself."

Porter heard another click come from the backseat as a wall of dark trees came right at them. Skip cut back just in time. The car shuddered as the wheels howled to hold the road.

"Damn, Skip!" Red screamed with delight. The mad ride had obviously pumped up his adrenalin. "You can flat out drive this vehicle, bro!"

"That sound fair to you or what?" Skip asked Porter.

Porter choked back suppressed nausea as he watched rabbit guts slip off the windshield and blow away into the night.

Then his little black book come flying over his shoulder. He grabbed instinctively for it, but it bounced off his knee and fell to the car floor. He bent down to pick it up and felt a sharp pain in the back of his head.

Red was squeezing the top of his neck, pushing it forward, until he had Porter's face pushed into the car's dirty, frayed carpeting.

"We ain't got all night," Skip added as Red bounced Porter's head off the car floor.

Porter's glasses popped off. He groped for them with one hand and the little black book with the other. The carpet smelled of stale beer and old cigarette butts.

"So what do you say, boy?" Skip shouted, kicking Porter in the head, hard.

Porter cried out in pain.

"What'd he say, Red?"

"I think he said he's thinking it over," Red replied, banging Porter's head off the filthy carpet a few more times.

"So what do you say, partner?" Skip asked.

Red yanked Porter back up.

Porter's head was now spinning. He felt carsick. But he wasn't going to let these jerks intimidate him. He knew once you caved in to bullies, they never let you alone.

Skip turned off the radio, and there was a deathly quiet in the car. "So what do you say?" Skip repeated, impatiently.

"Ah . . . think maybe you could call my secretary in the morning?" Porter deadpanned. "We'll do lunch."

"Hey, Red," Skip growled, mashing the gas peddle

to the floor. The car shot through the night, dark and deadly.

"I think we got a wiseass in the car. Let's get rid of him!"

Three

Skip flattened the brake pedal and the brakes locked up, sending the car into a shuddering skid. The car jolted to a halt. Red flung the passenger-side door open, sending a rush of cool air across Porter's face. He grabbed Porter and tossed him out of the car like a sack of potatoes.

"You've got one night to think about our little business proposition!" Skip snarled through the open door. *"One* night!" Red slammed the car door and the black Thunderbird roared away.

Porter rose shakily to his feet. He was back in the Night Owl parking lot, he noticed. He slipped his glasses on, which he was still clutching in his hand, and looked around for his black book. He found it sitting in the middle of an oil slick on the grungy parking lot ground. He carefully wiped it off and stuck it back in his pocket. Then he made his way slowly to his car.

He jumped into his battered '83 Oldsmobile and cranked over the ignition. The big motor rumbled to life and Porter drove out of the Night Owl parking lot onto Thirteen Bends Road and made his way back to the academy.

He swore under his breath.

Porter prided himself on being able to look down the road to foresee problems like this. All part of playing the angles. He shouldn't have allowed himself to be caught off guard like that.

Well, if those creeps thought they could mess with him they were playing a dangerous game. He'd had similar problems in the past, and he knew how to deal with them. He'd have to bring in the heavy artillery, that's all. Let those two slime balls deal with some major league muscle, Porter thought, watching his car light shine off the canopied tree tops.

It was time to make Tommy a player.

None of this would've happened if Tommy had been with him. Tommy was more than just Porter's roommate—he was his protection.

Porter wasn't the most popular guy at the academy, to say the least. He was a wiseguy and a poor institution man. He hated the Hudson Military Academy and its pretentious traditions. But what really rubbed his fellow cadets the wrong way was the salt he smeared into their wounds after taking them for their money. He might be a sports geek but he knew how to talk trash when it came to money.

Which was where Tommy came in. Tommy Wilson was the closest thing Porter had to a friend. Tommy was handsome in a roguish, dumb way that so many girls seemed to like. The only thing he and Porter seemed to have in common was that they were both on scholarship. Tommy was the academy's most prized slab of beef. Captain of the football team and star power forward on the basketball team. Not just content to squash quarterbacks on the gridiron or set crushing picks on the basketball court; he also loved boxing, wrestling, karate—any sport that could do serious damage to the human body.

Unfortunately, hanging out with Tommy only accentuated Porter's shortcomings when it came to physique. At six-foot-one, Porter was tall enough for basketball, but so skinny he would be ground to a pulp in a matter of minutes. He had tried to bulk up, lifting weights with Tommy at the gym, but it was no use. He was better at pushing pencils than push-ups, and he was smart enough to know that was where his best chances of success were.

Porter and Tommy had gone to middle school together. Porter had known right away that Tommy, a typical jock—big on brawn, small on brains—would be useful to have around. Just the type Porter would need to call friend if the opportunity ever presented itself. He saw his opening when he realized that Tommy had about as much chance of passing a math test as Porter himself had of making the football team. So Porter sat next to Tommy and let him copy off his test paper. Tommy never failed a math test after that.

In fact, Tommy never failed anything again when he and Porter took the same class.

Tommy tried to reciprocate by teaching Porter some self-defense techniques, but Porter preferred to let Tommy do the fighting for him.

It wasn't till after they both won scholarships to the Hudson Military Academy that Porter put his talents to work and started taking bets, and Tommy became addicted to gambling.

And Tommy *never* won. He was constantly into Porter for money. Which made it even easier for Porter to manipulate him. Porter often dropped Tommy's gambling debts in exchange for favors, such as slapping down certain cadets when they got out of line, or breaking a little finger when one of them tried to welch on a bet.

His classmates at the Hudson Military Academy quickly learned that if you messed with Porter Smith, you messed with Tommy Wilson. And messing with Tommy was a good way to get your face rearranged. Porter knew that without muscle backing him up, a scrawny kid like himself wouldn't stay in business for long. So when the going got tough, Porter got Tommy.

But that night Tommy and the basketball team had traveled upstate for a big away game against Roosevelt Academy; they wouldn't be back until tomorrow night.

Tomorrow night, when Porter would be at the Night Owl doing business again.

Tomorrow night, when Porter was supposed to meet the Jagger brothers and give them his decision.

He'd give them a decision all right—a six-foot-five decision.

Saturday night

Back at the Night Owl, Porter squirmed in his seat at the booth. He glanced at his watch. It was a half hour before curfew and Porter didn't think Tommy was going to make it. Now he'd have to get to his car on his own and risk running into those psychos again.

He decided it would be safer to bypass the parking lot and take the trail through the woods back to the academy. He could pick his car up tomorrow. Or send Tommy for it.

Well, if that was the way he was going, then he'd better go now. He stood up at the same time Skip Jagger burst into the room and looked in his direction with those creepy, pink eyes.

Before Skip could fix him in his sights, Porter dove beneath the booth table.

He felt his eyes glazing over from the heavy smell of the ammonia on the freshly mopped floor, and he fought back the urge to sneeze.

He watched a pair of legs come his way and cringed. Those motorcycle boots could do some serious damage to his face. He hoped Skip Jagger wouldn't beat him to a pulp right there in the Night Owl in front of all his classmates, who would enjoy nothing more than seeing him get his ass kicked.

"Yo!"

Porter moved farther beneath the table.

"Yo!" The voice above the table shouted down at Porter again. A girl's voice.

Porter peered out from beneath the table and saw a pretty girl about his age looking down at him with bright, curious brown eyes. She had on a tight, heavy metal T-shirt beneath a motorcycle jacket several sizes too large for her, which didn't hide the fact from Porter that she was also braless. She looked as if she had been poured into her jeans. Her shaggy brown hair was windswept around her face, even in the still atmosphere of the Night Owl.

"What are you doing down there?"

"Shhh—he's looking for me!" Porter whispered.

"Who's looking for you?" she asked in a normal tone of voice.

"Shhh!"

She continued to stand above him, her gaze boring down into him.

"Sit down and stop staring!" Porter whispered harshly.

"Huh?"

"Just sit down, okay?"

She sat down at the booth keeping a wary eye on Porter beneath the table. "Don't try anything funny down there," she warned.

"I won't," Porter said, although he wished her shirt wasn't so tight or he might have a chance of seeing something when he looked up at her. "What's your name?"

"Jamie. Jamie O'Reilly."

"My name's Porter Smith." Porter reached his hand up as he introduced himself. She looked at it quizzically before bending down a little to shake it.

"Glad to meet you," she said.

"Uh, now that we've officially met, uh could you do me a little favor. Just take a look around and tell me if you see a mean looking guy with spiky blond hair wearing a full length black leather jacket?"

"A guy with a dice earring?"

"Yeah."

"No. He's not up here."

33

"Very funny," Porter said in an annoyed tone of voice.

"I'm not kidding. He's not here. I saw him when I came in but he—wait. He just came back in." She paused. "Now he's sitting at the bar."

Porter peeked above the table top. Skip was sitting with his back to him. He scrambled out from beneath the table.

"Why is he looking for you?"

"He wants to kill me," Porter said as he sprinted from the table. He made his way through the crowded back rooms and opened the back door.

Standing just outside, and staring him in the face, was Red Jagger.

"Oh, hi, Red." Porter said, trying to get around the big, burly red-head. "Skip's inside. I think he's looking for you."

Red yanked Porter through the door and twisted his arm behind his back. Skip hurried out the back door. "Got 'em?"

"Oh, yeah," Red said. "I got him good." Red lifted Porter off the ground by his twisted arm. The pain shot from his shoulder up his back, and Porter yelped.

"Hey, take it easy, there, Red," Porter said in a light tone of voice, trying to conceal his fear.

The T-Bird rolled up beside them with Booger at the wheel. Booger moved over as Skip slid into the driver's seat. Red threw Porter into the backseat and crawled in after him. The Thunderbird ripped out of the parking lot.

"I told you I'd flush him out," Skip said with a wide grin, glancing over his shoulder as Porter struggled to escape. "Like a little scared rabbit out of his hole."

Porter instinctively looked at the windshield for traces of the rabbit they had hit the night before, but the windshield was clean.

The T-Bird stopped at the exit of the parking lot to let a car pass and Porter bolted for the opposite door. Red grabbed him and pulled him back. "He must not like me," Red said, putting a headlock on Porter. "Maybe it's my breath."

"Don't you like my brother?" Skip asked.

Porter couldn't answer if he wanted to. Red's choke hold was cutting off his air supply.

"Cat's got his tongue again, Skip," Red said.

Skip reached back and savagely tweaked Porter's nose, bringing tears to his eyes. "Answer me!" Skip bellowed.

Red squeezed harder. Porter groaned.

"Lighten up a second, Red. I think he's trying to say something."

Red loosened his choke hold. Porter gasped for breath. "Fellas," Porter croaked, rubbing his throat. "We have got to stop meeting this way."

Red slammed Porter face down on the backseat and wrapped a gag around his mouth. "You were right, Skip, he's a wiseguy, all right."

"And what do we do to wiseguys?" Skip asked Red, ominously, as he turned the radio on.

Rock screamed from the speakers.

"Use 'em for target practice," Red replied with a sadistic smile.

Four

The black Thunderbird shot through the night, down the twisting, windy Thirteen Bends Road. "Hey Red?" Skip shouted over his shoulder to his brother. "Remember that time we hung that dude upside down from the cliff edge, up there by lover's lane?"

"Yep," Red said, nodding and giggling. "Cat had his tongue, too," Red said as he tied Porter's hands behind his back.

"If I remember correctly, you sneezed and lost your grip and the clown just nose dived into the wild blue yonder."

"Oh yeah, that's right!" Red snapped the knot tight on the rope. "Remember the way he was flapping his arms like a bird on the way down?"

Porter winced as the bristly hairs of the rough rope cut deep into the bare skin of his wrists.

"That was almost as much fun as the time we took that dude to the meat packing plant—"

"Yeah, yeah, with the hooks," Red broke in, excited at the memory. "The big hooks they put the cows on, the dead cows . . ." Red lost himself in a spasm of giggles.

Skip joined the laughter. "Oh man, I wish I could've seen the plant manager's face when he stepped into the freezer the next morning and found that dude just hanging there . . ."

"Prime cut!" Red exclaimed.

Both brothers erupted into hysterical laughter. Booger remained silent in the front seat.

Porter wondered if the Jagger brothers were on something. These guys weren't normal, not even close.

Porter clenched his teeth behind the gag and fought back the panic rising inside of him. Either these two guys were jerking him around royally, or they were a couple of homicidal maniacs.

As they continued their morbid reminiscences, Porter listened and squirmed in the backseat. Skip was driving like a lunatic again. Porter made up his mind to make a break for it the next time the car stopped, even if he was gagged and had his hands tied behind his back.

Skip suddenly shut off the blaring rock music. Oddly, Porter found the silence in the car more threatening than the punk music that was crushing his eardrums just a few seconds before. The car slowed as Skip pulled over, stopped, and cut the lights.

Porter gulped. It was now or never. He eyed the opened back window and tried to find something to brace his feet on, to push off from. It was time for his human torpedo act.

But before he got a chance to try, Red grabbed

him by the rope and pulled him out of the car. He fell in a heap and Red had to stand him up. Porter saw they were parked next to the long stone wall that surrounded the academy. He remembered what Red said about using him for target practice and conjured up a vision of a two-man firing squad with him as the target.

But Red stepped up on the hood of the car, then the roof. He peeked over the top of the old stone wall, then crawled over it. Porter heard him drop with a soft thud on the other side. Skip nudged Porter. "Up and over it, twerp."

Porter climbed up on the car hood, roughly assisted by Skip, and slid over the wall. Red half caught him as he fell. Porter banged his shoulder on the ground, but at least he didn't break his neck. He had a premonition that before the night was over, he might prefer a quick death, like a broken neck, over what the Jaggers had in mind.

Red yanked Porter to his feet. Porter watched a length of rope come arcing over the wall, followed by Skip, who crashed to the ground with a grunt. Skip clambered to his feet, muttering a curse, and picked up the loose coil of rope. "I'm getting too old for this," he said to no one in particular.

"You're only twenty-two," Red said, grinning like a moron.

"Yeah, but I'm over a hundred inside my head."

It was then that Porter noticed Skip's dilated pupils in the gleam of the moonlight.

Speed freak.

Porter remembered Tommy telling him that half the basketball team used speed at one time or another, especially when they had a game after a long night of partying. He told Porter it was easy to tell which guys were on it, just look into their eyes. At their pupils. They'll be moving around like they have a life of their own.

Like Skip's eyes.

He watched Skip coiling up the extra rope and tried not to think what they would use it for. Booger stayed with the car, and the brothers quickly led Porter across the grassy expanse of the compound to a chorus of shrieking crickets.

The Jaggers seemed to know where they were going, Porter noted, although he seriously doubted they had ever attended the academy. He seriously doubted if they had even made it through grade school. They each held one of Porter's arms as they trotted Porter in the direction of— Suddenly, Porter knew.

The firing range.

What blood was left in Porter's face drained away. They were taking him to the firing range. They were going to tie his legs with the extra rope and leave him behind the row of big, cardboard targets. When the cadets arrived at the shooting range for target practice the next morning he'd be a sitting duck.

Porter ripped his arms free and made a break for it, hoping to attract the attention of the guard. He tried to scream, but the gag muffled the sounds so they were barely audible.

He didn't get far. Red caught up to him and punched him on the side of his head with his fist, knocking Porter to the ground. His head felt as if someone had just slammed a door on it. By the time he regained his senses Red was hog-tying him in the dirt trench behind the long row of target practice markers.

Red finished his task and Porter's arms and legs were now tightly tied behind his back, his mouth gagged even more tightly this time. The end of the rope was looped around his neck.

Skip sat nearby on a mound of dirt, his breath coming in sharp intakes. He pulled a small pint bottle out of his back pocket, uncapped it, and took a long drink. "Oh yeah, baby, that does take off the edge." He passed the bottle to Red.

Red took a hit and poured a little on Porter just for the hell of it.

"Hey, don't waste good whiskey on that little punk," Skip scolded in a low voice, reaching for the bottle.

Red gave him back the bottle and ripped Porter's wallet out of his pocket. He removed the cash and tossed the wallet to the ground. Porter watched the wind blow his American Express Gold Card away.

"We can buy a whole case of liquor with this." Red held up a fist full of cash. "Man, this little twerp is carrying around some kind of serious lettuce. Well . . . he won't be needing it." Red gave Skip half the money and stuffed the other half into his pocket. "Not after tonight."

Porter gave up. "Okay, guys, you win this round. I surrender." He grunted behind the gag, wanting to be heard.

Skip pocketed the money and took another hit from the bottle. "Hey Red? I think G.I. Joe wants to say something."

Red yanked the gag down taking a piece of Porter's lip with it.

"You got something you want to say to us?" Skip asked, his eyes wide with expectation.

There was a lot Porter would have liked to say, but he had to think of something that would get him out of this mess alive. He forced himself to smile, and he tasted blood. "Okay, partners! How about a fifty-fifty split."

Red laughed. "The little creep's got spunk, I'll say that much. I don't know, Skip . . . maybe this isn't such a good idea."

Porter breathed a sigh of relief. There was hope. He might still be able to reason with these two imbeciles.

"I think you're right, Red," Skip said. "If we leave him here someone might come along and find him. Let's go back to the car and get that five gallon can of gasoline and make us a bonfire."

Five

Red roughly gagged Porter as Skip took one last hit from the pint of whiskey. He threw the empty bottle at Porter, which bounced inches from his head and ricocheted out of sight. Then Skip and Red disappeared into the dark of the night, the quiet broken only by the crickets and Skip's loud belch.

Porter lay on his side on the cool, lumpy dirt of the trench and tried to remember how he had gotten into this situation so he could be sure never to do it again. What had happened?

He had just been minding his own business, doing a little nickel and dime bookmaking at the Night Owl Club, and now this. Like he had been caught in a bad dream and couldn't wake up. Except this was no dream. Porter felt a chill down to his bones at the savage reality of his situation. He could die. Tonight.

Horribly. Painfully.

He struggled to loosen the ropes, but Red had tied the rope so tightly it was cutting off his circulation. His body felt like one big cramp. And when he struggled, the noose around his neck tightened. But if he didn't get free and get his blood moving again, he'd die from lack of circulation.

Porter made a promise to himself to kill Tommy if he lived through this. It was all Tommy's fault.

Tommy *always* came to the Night Owl after a big game. What were the odds that he wouldn't make it there that night, of all nights? He should've been there. Porter hadn't realized how dependant he had become on Tommy.

Porter struggled to free himself again but quickly gave it up when the noose around his neck tightened even more, choking off his air. Red might be a moron, but he sure knew his knots.

Porter heard footsteps coming his way followed by another loud belch. They were back already. Back to set him on fire. He didn't even have time to watch his life pass before his eyes.

The footsteps were now in the trench.

Porter was sweating bullets. He sensed a presence above him, looking down, breathing hard. "Little buddy, why the hell are you tied up behind the firing range?"

It was Tommy. Thank God!

Tommy often called Porter his "little buddy." Porter usually called him "big guy." Porter realized Tommy must be sneaking back to their room; it was probably after curfew.

Tommy untied Porter and removed the bloody gag. Porter stood up shakily. His arms and legs tingled as the blood started to flow freely through his veins.

"What the hell happened to you?" Tommy asked, sitting down clumsily on the cold ground. Porter could tell he had done some serious partying that night. He could smell Tommy's breath from where he stood. "Jesus, you stink. You smell like I feel."

Porter gently massaged his wrists and throat, which were rubbed raw from the tight ropes. "Where were you tonight ya' big lummox?" Porter asked in an annoyed voice. "You were supposed to be at the Night Owl." It felt good to be able to release some of his anger and frustration, even though it was at Tommy and not the Jaggers.

Tommy's handsome face clouded over in confusion. "I was?"

"The team always goes there after a big game."

"Sorry, Mom," Tommy said sarcastically. "But I was into something else."

"What?" Porter asked curtly, still annoyed.

"Some girl's pants."

"Huh?" Porter stooped to pick up his empty wallet and felt a muscle spasm in his back.

Tommy seemed oblivious to his friend's pain. "We creamed Roosevelt Academy so bad we felt sorry for them. So me and a couple of the guys on the team decided to stay behind and cheer up their cheerleaders. You know what a great humanitarian I am."

"Yeah, yeah," Porter said, half-listening, looking inside his wallet. The Jaggers had taken all of his cash and his American Express Gold Card had blown away. He didn't carry any pictures.

Tommy was clearly disappointed Porter wasn't more interested in his latest conquest. The three most important things in his life were the academy, sports, and girls. Although not necessarily in that order. "I scored, buddy. Aren't you going to congratulate me?"

Tommy lay back on the bare ground with a smug look on his face and yawned contentedly.

Porter hated to admit it, but he envied the hell out of Tommy. The guy had probably been laid more often his senior year at HMA than Porter would in his entire life. If he *ever* managed to get laid. Tommy was something else with the ladies. He didn't even want to think of what Tommy's success rate might be if he went to a school that *had* girls.

"Congratulations," Porter said halfheartedly, searching for his Gold Card in the moonlight. He was more concerned with what to do about the Jaggers than he was with Tommy's sexual adventures.

He gave up looking for the card. He'd cancel it tomorrow. He never used it anyway. He just liked the girls from the Cooper Riding Academy to see it when he opened his wallet at the Night Owl. Which he found was about as effective a way of getting laid as wiggling his ears.

The Jaggers had cleaned him out and there wasn't a thing he could do about it, either. He couldn't exactly go to the police without explaining how he had gotten all that money in the first place. He'd have to go to the bank tomorrow and withdraw a little cash.

He looked at Tommy, already snoring. "Tommy!"

"Hmmm?"

"How much money do you owe me?"

"Ah, Porter," Tommy mumbled in a sleepy voice. "Let me slide until next week. You know I'm good for it, you know that, little buddy . . ." his voice trailed off as he slipped back into a drunken stupor.

"You can get it down to nothing if you do me a little favor."

Tommy's eyes flared open. "What little favor?"

Porter glanced at his watch. It was *way* past curfew. They'd better get back to their room before the guard caught them.

Or before the Jaggers returned.

"C'mon, I'll explain back at the room."

Sunday night

Porter sat nervously by himself at his booth in the Night Owl and tried to fight back the sick feeling that had been yanking at his intestines all night long. It was a sleepless night he'd spent listening to Tommy snore while trying to figure out what to do.

He had evaluated all of the options at least five times, and as much as he hated to admit it, going in with the Jaggers was the best available one. For the moment, at least. Until he came up with something better.

It was one thing to get Tommy to slap some guys around. But the Jaggers were obviously creeps of a different dimension. It would take more than a little slapping to get them to leave him alone. A lot more, Porter feared. It would probably take some bone-breaking persuasion—an arm or a leg. Possibly even a neck if things got totally out of hand.

Porter didn't think he had the stomach for that kind of violence. Although he suspected Tommy would have gladly taken on the task to wipe away more gambling debts. Which was why he found the big lug so useful.

Tommy walked into the crowded room and caught

Porter's eye. He gave Porter the prearranged signal—the Jaggers had arrived at the Night Owl and would probably be making their way over to the bar. Then he took a seat at the bar himself where he could keep an eye on things.

Porter kept his eyes glued to the door and waited for the Jaggers to come into the room. Despite Tommy's presence, Porter felt uneasy, and couldn't completely quell the bad feeling he'd had ever since he had made his decision to go in with hairballs like the Jaggers. But now there was something else bothering him. He couldn't quite put his finger on it. Something else was tugging away at his conscience.

He looked up and saw Jenny Demos staring at him again.

Was it his imagination or did her face actually seem to be glowing. He felt a throbbing in his head and felt his cheeks grow warm like he was sitting with his face to the sun on a hot summer day. He put his hand up as if to block an invisible beam. The throbbing slowly subsided.

Weird.

He looked back at the door and his heart shot into his throat—the Jaggers had just walked into the room. He had to resist the temptation to dive beneath the table again. Skip did a double take when he saw Porter. He jabbed Red in the ribs and pointed in the direction of the booth. Red grinned that moronic grin that went so perfectly with the rest of his face. The Jaggers strutted over and slid into the booth opposite Porter.

"How'd you get loose, anyway?" Skip asked. "Red

brought back marshmallows and everything. We were going to have a regular cookout."

"Never mind that, let's take care of this business first," Porter said, working up a tough guy tone of voice. As if escaping death for him was an everyday occurrence. He looked over Skip's shoulder to make certain Tommy hadn't seen some cute girl and wandered off. "First of all, no more rough stuff."

Skip only shrugged. "That's up to you." He pulled out a small pair of ivory dice and shook them around inside his hand. The rattling noise unnerved Porter for a second, but he quickly recovered. He knew he had to keep his focus, or he was doomed.

"So what's your offer?" Porter asked.

"It's like I said the other night, we'll back you financially so you can raise the ante on your bets. From now on all bets are over twenty bucks. I know them rich kids at the academy got it. Or can be *persuaded* to get it if they get a little behind. That's where me and Red come in. It's easy. All you've got to do is open up your operation a little by raising your stakes."

"And what's the break?" Porter wondered if the Jaggers would keep cleaning him out the way they had just taken all his money the previous night.

"Fifty-fifty," Skip said.

Porter shook his head skeptically. "No way. I'd lose money."

"According to my bookkeeper, Mr. Boogers, you won't. But even if that happened, there are other ways to make up the difference."

"What other ways?" Porter asked curiously.

Skip smirked as he rolled his dice around in his

hand. "Never mind that, let's take care of *this business first,*" he said, mimicking Porter's words of a few moments before. "Do we have a deal or what?"

Porter knew he didn't have much of a choice. "All right, I'm in," he said in a resigned tone of voice.

Skip slapped Red on the arm with the back of his hand. Red pulled a plain paper bag out of his jacket pocket and tossed it to Porter. "Remember what I said, no bets under twenty dollars. We'll see you at the end of the week to collect our share—*partner.*" The Jaggers got up to leave.

Porter didn't bother shaking their hands. When the Jaggers were out of sight, he held the bag beneath the table and counted the money. There was over a thousand dollars in cash! The most Porter had ever carried around with him was a few hundred dollars. He didn't lose often enough to carry any more than that. Carrying this much money was already making him nervous. He thought of giving it to Tommy but was afraid he might bet it on something before they even got back to their room.

And he'd better not lose it, Porter realized, or Red might still get his barbecue. If they didn't run him down in their car first.

A long dark shadow cast over the booth table, making Porter look up with a start. It was Tommy. He slid in next to Porter. "What's up, little buddy?"

Porter explained to him the terms of the partnership. "Did you recognize those two guys?" he asked.

"I've seen them around here the last couple of weeks, but I don't know where they're from. I can check around a little though, if you want."

Porter nodded, and Tommy left.

Porter got up to leave. He stuffed the bag of money inside his jacket, patted it to make sure it wouldn't fall out, and headed for the arched doorway across the room.

Porter felt that funny, tugging feeling again. He glanced over his shoulder right into the eyes of Jenny Demos, who was standing behind the bar. A rush of goosebumps bathed his body. He changed directions and went out a different door.

It was weird. He never went this way.

Porter passed an arched doorway that led to one of the game rooms. Porter heard shouting coming from one of the rooms and looked in. He saw the girl who had come over to his table the night before and tried to remember her name.

Janie, no, Jamie.

She was arguing with someone.

Porter stopped to get a better look.

Just in time to see Jamie throw a bright green pool ball at Reggie Reeves.

Six

The ball struck Reggie in the chest with a thud. Reggie staggered backward until his back hit the sturdy mahogany pool table. He leaned against the table and gasped for breath.

She was just as pretty as Porter remembered her to be. Even prettier, in fact, now that she was angry. She was wearing a black tank top over the same tight jeans. The black leather jacket she had worn the night before was tossed carelessly over a nearby chair. She was braless again.

Jamie pointed an accusing finger at Reggie. "You lost! Now pay!" Porter smiled. So he and the girl had something in common after all. They both collected from Reggie.

"You didn't call your shot," Reggie croaked, rubbing his chest as if he was checking to see if the ball had left an indentation. "I don't owe you a damn thing," he said more forcefully.

"Where I come from we don't have to call our shots!"

"Well I don't know where you come from, but in

the Night Owl we do," Reggie said, keeping a wary eye on the enraged girl just in case she tried to poke his eye out with a cue stick. "Besides, you were just lucky. You could never beat me in a hundred years."

She picked up another pool ball. "You pay me or you're going to have matching lumps you creep!"

"You throw another pool ball at me, and I'm going to slap your teeth right out of your mouth!"

Leave it to Reggie to pick a fight with a girl, Porter thought, stepping between them. "Cool it guys, come on. Stop already, huh?"

Porter didn't normally play the role of peacemaker. Usually when a fight broke out, he took off in the other direction. But Jamie had helped him out the other night. Not to mention that she also was wearing the cutest little tank top he had ever seen painted on to a girl. This wasn't the way he thought he'd meet the girl of his dreams—breaking up a fight between her and a cadet. But he was up for whatever it took to make a good impression.

Porter looked at Reggie and shook his head. "You cheating on your bets again, Reg?"

"This is between me and her, so butt out butt-head!"

A crowd was gathering.

"Well, now, that's very brave of you to pick a fight with a *girl*," Porter said, playing a little to the crowd. He looked at Reggie, who swayed a little, and suspected he'd had a few beers before coming to the Night Owl. "What a man, what a man," Porter said, clucking his tongue at Reggie in disgust.

Some chuckles came out of the crowd.

"Kick her ass, pal," came a sarcastic voice directed at Reggie.

"I don't fight girls," Reggie said, his face turning crimson. He glared at Porter. "But why don't *you* and *me* step out into the parking lot right now."

Porter felt all the eyes in the room turn in his direction, waiting expectantly for Porter to take up the challenge. But Porter had never been in a fight in his life. He had been beaten up a few times, but he didn't count those as fights, since he never fought back. Tommy had even taught him some boxing and karate, but Porter had never been able to actually use it in a fight. He just didn't have the killer instinct. He usually covered up the best he could and waited for his opponent to get bored.

But this situation was a little different. He didn't want to be humiliated in public, In front of his classmates. In front of Jamie.

"Fight!" came a mocking voice from the crowd. "Porter Smith's gonna get his ass kicked!" Porter suspected the voice had come from a cadet who probably owed him money.

A few more voices joined in. "Fight! Fight!" the chant began.

This wasn't supposed to have happened, Porter thought. He swallowed hard and searched the sea of faces. Where was Tommy when he needed him?

"C'mon wimp," Reggie said, grabbing Porter by the lapel of his denim jacket. "Let's step outside—"

"I don't need anyone to fight my fights for me," Jamie said, roughly slapping Reggie's hand away from Porter's jacket. *"I'll* meet you outside."

Laughter erupted from the crowd as Reggie sputtered in anger.

Porter admired her spunk—or maybe she just felt sorry for him—but he wished she'd shut up! She was just making it worse.

"Either pay me what you owe me or step outside," Jamie said, looking Reggie in the eyes. This girl doesn't give up, Porter thought with admiration. And Porter believed she would go through with it, too.

"I could beat you, blindfolded," Reggie said, looking nervously at the faces in the crowd.

"Then rack 'em up and let's do it again," Jamie challenged.

"I don't want to take your money, little girl," Reggie said, rubbing talc on his hands. As far as he was concerned, the conversation was over.

"You're just chicken," she said.

A titter of laughter came from the crowd.

"Why don't you put your money where your mouth is," Porter said. "I've got two hundred bucks that says she can beat you."

"Let's see it," Reggie demanded.

"It's in your pocket," Porter replied.

"Huh?"

"You owe me two hundred."

"Since when?"

"Since the Lakers upset the Knicks at the Garden last night."

"Oh . . ." Reggie mumbled. He thought about it for a moment as he chalked up his pool stick. "Let's make it double or nothing," he said with a condescending smile as he blew chalk dust into Porter's face.

A buzz went through the crowd.

Porter wiped the dust from his face. He was as angry as he had ever been in his life. He pulled the brown paper bag out of his jacket and emptied the contents on the pool table. "Let's make it a thousand!"

A louder buzz went through the crowd.

"You're on," Reggie said, ramming a quarter into the pool stable change slot and yanking back a handle. The balls fell with a clunk and rolled back to his side of the table, where he retrieved them.

A little voice inside Porter's head said something to him—it sounded like "sucker." If he had taken the time to explore the angles, he would have seen that it was a chump bet against steep odds. A bet made on impulse, on emotion—a sucker's bet.

But it was too late to do anything about it.

Seven

The crowd suddenly parted as a tall thin man with a mane of snowy white hair seemed to appear out of nowhere. It was Jake Demos, Jenny's father. Jake was tall and angular with a forehead that seemed too large for the rest of his head. His nose was long and hooked enough to open a can, Porter thought. He had a scary look about him, especially his eyes, the eyes of a hawk zeroing in on its prey.

"What's all the commotion—" he began before he saw the money spread out all over the pool table. Jake curiously wiped his hands off on a stained apron as his eyes scanned the room. "I've heard of money growing on trees but not out of pool tables."

A few giggles came out of the crowd. The tension in the air abated somewhat.

"So where'd all this money come from?" Jake asked.

Porter, who was standing closest to the money, started scooping it up self-consciously. "Sorry about that, sir. I was . . . er . . . just collecting money for some charity—multiple sclerosis. You know, Jerry's kids. We're very close to a breakthrough. Very close."

Jake just scratched his beak-like nose with a bony finger, obviously not believing a word of what Porter was saying. He watched Porter shovel the money back into the brown paper bag before bending over to pick up the pool ball that Jamie had bounced off Reggie. He gingerly placed the ball back on the pool table. Porter stuffed the last of the bills into the paper bag and shoved it into his denim jacket.

Jake looked at Porter, at his haircut. "Are you one of the cadets from the academy?"

"Yes, sir," Porter replied, buttoning up his jacket.

Jake nodded. "Well . . . carry on." He gave Porter a little mock salute before returning to the kitchen.

The crowd, which had smelled blood just a few moments earlier, slowly dispersed and melted away. The sounds of laughter and boisterous conversation picked up again.

Then Porter saw Tommy walking his way. "Some bodyguard you are," Porter said. "What the hell am I paying you for?"

"Why, what happened?" Tommy asked defensively. "I thought the Jaggers left."

"Never mind," Porter said. "Did you find out anything about them?"

"Plenty," Tommy said. "Let's go some place where we can talk in private." They found an empty table in a dark corner. When they were settled in Tommy whispered, "Those guys are really bad news."

"Tell me something I don't know." Porter took a deep breath, trying to calm his frayed nerves.

"They went to Cooper Hollow High a few years

ago. They had their own little bookmaking operation going there for a while. Since it didn't look like they would ever graduate, or even wanted to, they were finally just kicked out of school. They moved to New York City and set up shop downtown on the Lower East Side."

"Making book?"

"Yeah, at first, but then they started to get into some heavier stuff."

"Like what?"

"Drugs. You know: pot, coke, crack, stuff like that. Crystal meth."

"Crystal meth? That's speed, isn't it?" Porter asked, remembering the way Skip's eyes looked the night before.

"The worst," Tommy said. "It's addictive and totally rots your brain. You'd really have to be insane to stay on that stuff any length of time. Anyway, they started out dealing it, but ended up doing most of it themselves. They ended up owing their suppliers a lot of money they couldn't pay back."

Porter was catching on. "So they came running back here."

"You would, too, if you were being chased by a biker gang from the Lower East Side. It's a club called the Holy Savages. They were the Jaggers' main supplier. The biker leader was this real big guy named Sonny "Meat Bomb" Barker. He was part of a drug bust or something. I think he's in jail now."

"Yeah, right, now I remember. It was in the paper a little while ago." Porter nodded his head. "So, those are the guys the Jaggers are involved with?"

"*Were* involved with," Tommy corrected. "Before

58

he got busted, Barker slapped around the Jaggers for not having his money. He gave the Jaggers twenty-four hours to come up with his money or he'd break their legs. The next night Barker sent his little brother for the dough, but he never came back. No one can prove it, but the Jaggers probably killed him."

Porter started to get a little nervous. If what Tommy was telling him was true—that the Jaggers were murderers—he was in bigger trouble than he had imagined. But just how reliable were Tommy's sources? A lot of guys liked to exaggerate.

"So Barker's sworn to hunt the Jaggers down and kill them both with his bare hands," Tommy continued. "And everyone in their gang."

"Everyone in their *gang?*"

"And from what I hear the guy can do it," Tommy went on. "He's supposed to be humongous. Bigger than me even. He's supposed to be so strong he can actually pick up a Harley. I mean, like *both* wheels off the ground," Tommy said with obvious admiration.

Porter wasn't interested in how much weight he could lift. "What's this about a gang?"

"Whatta you mean?"

"This Meat Bomb guy threatened to kill everyone in the Jagger's *gang.* The Jaggers don't have a gang. Unless you count Booger."

Tommy gave Porter a very serious look. "And you."

Porter looked at Tommy and swallowed hard.

Tommy laughed and clasped Porter on the shoulder with his big hand. "Just kidding. The Jaggers don't have a gang. Meat Bomb just doesn't know it, that's all. Besides, Meat Bomb's probably behind bars for the rest of his life. I wouldn't worry too much about him."

Porter shook his head. "This is a little more than—I thought they might be just jerking me around in the car with all those stories . . ."

"I don't know what stories they were telling you, but I'm pretty sure these Jaggers are about as low as scum can get." Tommy cracked his fingers, cool as a cucumber. "So . . . how do you want to handle it?"

"I—I don't know. I—I need some time to think about it." Porter was really shaken. His experiences didn't prepare him for negotiating with cold-blooded killers.

Tommy nodded his head. "Okay. Whatever you want to do is cool with me. I'm itching for a little action."

Tommy definitely had a mean streak in him, Porter knew, he had manipulated it often enough. Even under his jacket, his muscles seemed to be twitching. "Um . . . I'll talk to you later about it, all right?" Porter said.

"Right, boss." Tommy got up to leave, hesitated. "Hey—we're clear, right?"

"Huh?" Porter's asked, preoccupied with other matters.

"The slate's wiped clean. I'm off your books, right?"

"Oh . . . yeah, sure big guy, we're even."

"Cool," Tommy said. "Then put me down for twenty—no wait. You raised the stakes, right?"

"Yeah."

"Excellent. Then make it *fifty* on the Bucks-Suns game, okay bro?"

"Fifty?" Porter asked, a little surprised, automatically reaching for his little black book. He scribbled the bet down. "On the Suns?"

"No, the Bucks."

"You're kidding," Porter said derisively. It was a stupid bet, but Porter didn't know why he was telling Tommy that. Maybe taking his money had just become too easy, like taking candy from a baby. Or maybe his nerves were just so frayed, he didn't have any patience for Tommy's stupidity at the moment. "The Suns always beat the Bucks in Phoenix. Everyone knows that."

"I just got a feeling about this one," Tommy said confidently. "I think the Bucks are going to do it this time."

Porter shook his head and wrote down the information. "It's a loser bet. You're a loser, man. Always were." Porter shrugged. Tommy would just work his losses off later. And Porter had a feeling he would need him later.

There was an awkward silence.

Porter immediately realized that he had gone too far this time and really hurt Tommy's feelings calling him a loser. Even though that's what he was. "Sorry I called you a loser, man. It's just lately . . . I don't know . . ."

"Forget it," Tommy said, accepting Porter's flimsy apology. "Well, gotta go," Tommy said, snapping out of it. "I saw this really cute little tightbody in the other room. I thought I'd try to work my charms on her."

61

"Yeah?" Porter asked, feigning interest. He felt bad about calling Tommy a loser and wanted to make it up to him. He knew Tommy loved to talk about girls.

"Yeah. Did you see her? Over by the pool table. Dark shaggy hair, long legs, not to mention the nicest set of rib balloons I've seen in a long time." He was, of course, referring to Jamie.

Porter listened with a sickened feeling as Tommy actually smacked his lips. Porter felt a stab of jealousy and didn't know why, since he barely knew her.

"You know the one I mean?"

"Yeah, I know her," Porter said resigned. He could kiss any chance he thought he had with Jamie goodbye now that Tommy had her scent.

Tommy clapped a big meaty paw on Porter's bony shoulder, the awkwardness of a few moments before already forgotten. "Well, little buddy, I guess I'll see you back at the room later tonight. Unless, of course . . ." he gave Porter a playful little punch. "I get lucky."

Easy come, easy go, Porter thought, as he watched Tommy leave. He should be used to it by now. He made a conscious effort not to look into the billiards room when he walked past it. He didn't want to watch Tommy put the moves on Jamie, especially if she responded. Besides, he had to get back to the academy and lock up the money the Jaggers had given him before he got ripped off. Enough people had seen him dump it on the pool table, and one of them may have gotten the wrong idea. At least he wouldn't have to worry about the Jaggers ripping him off. It was, after all, their money.

Porter crossed the parking lot to his car, keeping his eyes open for potential trouble.

He was halfway across when he found it.

A dark figure walked out from behind the shadows of a pick up truck and came toward him.

Wearing a ski mask.

With a baseball bat dangling from his hand.

Eight

Porter turned and ran back toward Night Owl. He glanced over his shoulder and nearly freaked out when he saw that the figure was running toward him and gaining rapidly. As he ran, he judged the distance to the Night Owl and the speed of his pursuer and doubted if he would make it.

Then suddenly a motorcycle came careening out of the darkness from the opposite end of the parking lot. The roar of its engine cutting through the still night air startled Porter. He looked up, trapped in the glare of a single burning headlight, and watched helplessly as a big Harley-Davidson came right at him, apparently intent on tattooing a tread mark across his face. But instead the bike skidded to a stop in front of him. "Get on!" the rider barked.

Porter just stared, baffled.

"C'mon, let's go!" the rider said anxiously, revving the bike engine.

Porter glanced over his shoulder and saw that the figure with the baseball bat was only several yards away. Porter hopped on the back of the bike. The driver kicked in the clutch and gave the big bike plenty of throttle. They tore out of the parking lot, the front tire lifting off the ground as they shot away like a runaway bullet. The bike righted itself as it sped out of the parking lot and made a hairpin turn, nearly losing Porter in the process.

"Put your hands around my waist," the driver shouted back to Porter. "Unless you want your brains scrambled all over Thirteen Bends Road."

Porter did as he was told. Beneath the thick black leather of the motorcycle jacket, Porter felt hard stomach muscles tense and untense as the driver expertly shifted through the gears. He held on for his life as they went up and down, through and around Thirteen Bends Road.

Porter looked back only once, but he saw no one following them. He doubted if anyone could have kept up with them unless they were flying in a helicopter. They roared into town and pulled into the parking lot of the Bowl-A-Rama. Porter dismounted the bike unsteadily and looked curiously at his rescuer. He was so grateful, he didn't know what to say. The driver removed a bulky motorcycle helmet and turned toward Porter.

Porter's mouth dropped open in amazement.

"Are you all right?" Jamie asked, shaking out her dark shaggy hair that had gotten mashed beneath the motorcycle helmet. She was so self-assured, Porter felt stronger just being in her presence.

"Well, I—I . . ." Porter stammered. "Yeah, I think so. I may need a change of underwear, but . . ."

Jamie laughed loudly. "Sorry about that. I guess I do drive a little crazy, but it looked like that guy with the baseball bat meant business." She tugged off her leather riding gloves and tossed them in her empty helmet before unzipping her black leather jacket. Her helmet slipped and clattered to the ground.

"I guess I'm a little shaken up, too," Jamie said. Porter watched her bend over to pick up the helmet and impulsively grabbed her around the waist and hugged her. At first, Jamie was startled, but a moment later her body relaxed in Porter's strong embrace, and she lifted her face to his and kissed him. Then she wrapped her arms tightly around his back and pressed her body closer. Porter felt his senses spin.

"I like you," Jamie said, when her lips left his.

"And I like the way you show it," Porter said, hoping his inexperience wasn't too obvious. He tilted his head to meet hers, and this time their kiss was more passionate.

Jamie ran her hand up and down the front of Porter's shirt lingering at the buttons as if she were going to undress him right there in the parking lot.

Jamie licked the tip of Porter's nose playfully and pushed off from his chest.

"There's a little lunch counter in the Bowl-A-Rama if you want to grab a bite to eat," Jamie said casually. "I hear the burgers are great here."

Porter couldn't think of a way to move the conversation around to getting a room together, and there was a moment of awkward silence.

"Are you coming?" Jamie asked over her shoulder as she disappeared into the Bowl-A-Rama.

Porter hurried after her.

66

* * *

Porter watched Jamie work her way through her second Bowl-A-Rama Burger Deluxe, compliments of Porter. After all, she had saved his life. Porter didn't have much of an appetite. Just the thought of the man in the ski mask with the baseball bat was enough to make him sick to his stomach. He guessed he just wasn't cut out for rough stuff like this.

He watched Jamie spear another french fry and plunge it into a puddle of ketchup on her plate. He didn't know where she put it all, since there wasn't an ounce of fat on her body that he could see. And he had checked her out pretty thoroughly in the past few minutes.

Porter's hormones were definitely raging out of control. He had only dated a few times in his life and never gotten beyond the light necking stage. Usually with the ugly friends of Tommy's dates.

Of course, if he had Tommy's good looks and killer physique, Porter reasoned, he was sure he would have gone all the way with a girl by now. But the sad fact was that he was still a teenage virgin with the mind of a dirty old man.

So he watched Jamie eat, fantasized about what was underneath her tank top, and conjured up thoughts that would make sleep impossible that night.

Porter did a few mathematical equations in his head to ease the sexual tension. But even so, he felt more at ease with Jamie that he normally did with a girl. Maybe it was because she was as bold as he was shy. He felt no need to try and impress her. He hadn't even wiggled his ears for her one time that night. She was the perfect girl for a demented dork like himself, he thought.

"Sorry to eat like a pig, but I was really starving," Jamie said with a mouthful of food. "I missed dinner."

"Don't your parents feed you?"

"My parents live in Chicago, I just moved to Cooper Hollow. I'm staying with my uncle. Like most bachelors, the inside of his refrigerator looks like a science project. My uncle and his pals usually eat at places like this on their breaks. Cheap, but filling. That's how I found out about it."

"What does your uncle do?" Porter asked as she dug into the little white cup of coleslaw that came with the burger. She chased it down with her second cup of coffee before turning her captivating rich brown eyes on Porter.

"He's a cop."

Porter felt the blood drain from his face. His biggest fear was getting caught running his bookie operation. That would put an end to his money making machine not to mention most of his future plans. He avoided the police like the plague. Jamie seemed all right, but he didn't know about her uncle. Cops had a way of prying things out of people. Even nieces.

"Are you normally this pale or was it something I said?" Jamie asked.

"What kind of cop is your uncle?" Porter asked, hopefully. Maybe he was a traffic cop or something like that.

"You have a problem with the police?"

"Not yet."

Jamie smirked. "No offence, but you don't look like the criminal type to me."

"Just how many criminal types have you known, anyway?"

"Quite a few where I grew up actually. I ran with a pretty rough crowd, another reason my parents sent me to Cooper Hollow—to keep me out of trouble. I also have a bad habit of losing my temper."

Porter grinned. "I noticed." So had Reggie. "Did these criminal types teach you how to ride a motorcycle?"

"Ride 'em and fix 'em, too. I found that old Harley in my uncle's garage, getting rusty. It used to be a cop's hog. My uncle bought it cheap but never did anything with it. So I kind of took it over."

"Doesn't your uncle object to his niece blasting around Cooper Hollow on a retooled Harley with strange boys on the back?"

"You're the first boy I've taken for a ride since I've gotten here," she said with a sly smile. "As for my uncle, I guess he would object—if he knew."

"Smart move. You said 'one reason' you moved to Cooper Hollow? What were the other reasons?"

"My parents are in the middle of World War Three."

Porter gave her a quizzical look.

"Divorce."

Porter nodded knowingly. "So, you're going to Cooper Hollow High?"

"Yep. Just started my junior year. My parents thought Cooper Hollow might offer a more 'peaceful environment.'"

Porter laughed.

"What's so funny?" Jamie asked.

"Since I've met you—if you count hiding under the booth table at the Night Owl as our first meeting—I've been kidnapped, hog-tied, and left to die behind a shooting range. I broke up a fight between you and one of my classmates, almost got myself into a fight with the same guy, and nearly got my head bashed in with a baseball bat. That doesn't include being taken for a ride on a motorcycle that loosened a few of my brains cells. You call this peaceful?"

"It is compared to living with my parents," Jamie deadpanned. "Is it always this much fun around here? Or is it just because the moon is full?"

"Cooper Hollow's normally pretty tame. The most happening place is the Nightmare Club."

"The Nightmare Club?"

"I mean . . . the Night Owl Club. But everyone calls it the Nightmare Club," Porter explained.

"And why is that?"

Porter shrugged. "A lot of strange things seem to happen there. Haven't you noticed?"

"Well, I met you there, and you are pretty strange."

"Me?" He had just been thinking the same thing about her.

"I don't often meet guys hiding under tables."

She had him there. Porter said with mock-seriousness, "There's even a rumor that the Night Owl is . . . haunted."

Jamie grew wide-eyed. "Ooooooooooh," she said, making a spooky sound. "I am *so-o* scared."

"I doubt if anything scares you," Porter said sincerely. He admired her bravery.

"Why does everyone go there if it's supposed to be haunted?"

"That *is* why they go there," Porter said.

Jamie was quiet for a moment. "You wanna hear something funny, all joking aside? Remember when you were hiding beneath the table? This is going to sound weird, but I felt like I was sent over there."

"Sent to my table?"

"Yeah."

"But how could you see me under the table?"

"I couldn't. That's what I mean. I didn't even know about the Night Owl Club until that night. I was in my uncle's garage working on the bike when this flyer for the Night Owl Club blew in through the garage door and stuck to the spokes of the bike. I had been working all evening on the bike trying to get it to run without much luck. So I tried to kick-start it one more time and the damn thing came to life. I found the Night Owl and was chatting with this girl behind the bar when I had this weird sensation. In my head. I don't know exactly how to describe it . . ."

"Like a tugging at your brain?"

"Yeah!" Jamie said, fixing Porter with a stare. "Exactly. Does that ever happen to you?"

"Only at the Night Owl."

"The next thing I knew, I was walking over to your table. And there you were. Peeking out."

Porter smiled sheepishly.

"Did that guy really want to kill you?"

71

"Nah, I was just goofing around," Porter said. "I lost something and was looking for it?"

Jamie gave him a skeptical look. "Don't lie. You just gave me this whole story about being kidnapped and hog-tied and whatever else."

"I'll tell you about it later," Porter said. He changed the subject. "This woman you were talking to . . . was she a pretty woman with blond hair?"

"Uh, huh." Jamie nodded. "I remember her eyes, they were violet—very unusual."

Porter nodded. "They kind of stay with you, don't they?"

"Yeah. You know her?"

"Sort of. Her name is Jenny Demos. Her father runs the Night Owl. That spooky looking guy in the billiards room that made me put the money away."

The money. He had almost forgotten about it. He had a sudden, panic-filled moment that the money was gone. He had lost it somewhere in the parking lot of the Night Owl or on Thirteen Bends Road. He patted his denim jacket.

The money was still there. Porter sighed audibly with relief. Jamie noticed what he was doing and seemed disconcerted. "Where did you get all that money?" she asked. "And don't give me that crap about Jerry's kids."

Porter breathed out heavily. "All right, I'll tell you the truth . . . I was hiding from Reggie. He's wanted to kick my ass for a long time."

"For real?" Jamie asked.

"Yeah." Porter gave her a big wink. "I steal all his women."

Jamie smirked. "He has a dirty mouth. And he's

72

a cheat. Is that what they teach you at that academy? To be dirty-minded little cheats?"

Porter held up his hand in protest. "Absolutely not. We usually learn that on our own. The academy teaches us more useful skills, like how to take orders and kill people."

"Well, I think that big mouth at the pool table tried to rip you off in the parking lot?"

Porter raised his eyebrows. "Think so?"

"Don't you?"

Porter mulled it over. "I don't know. Maybe. Not that he needs the money—his parents have mucho bucks. He might do it just to drill me. They all hate me there."

"At the academy?"

"Yeah."

"Why?"

Porter shrugged. "They're a bunch of snobs. My family's blue-collar, theirs are gold Rolexed. It's like my being at the academy has somehow thrown a taint upon them all."

"You mean this Reggie guy was so tainted he wanted to take your head off with a baseball bat?"

Porter shrugged again. "I doubt if it was him. It was probably a townie punk who saw me dump all that money out on the pool table and thought he had an easy score. But, you know, that's what I get for acting like some macho moron."

"Oh, I don't know," Jamie said, fixing Porter with a seductive gaze. "I thought it was pretty cool."

"It was pretty *stupid* is what it was," Porter said, still pleased she had gotten a rise out of his chivalrous act.

"What's so stupid about—" Jamie batted her eyelashes "—sticking up for a lady?"

"Well, to begin with, in case you haven't noticed," Porter pointed out. "I'm not exactly Arnold Schwarzenegger."

"Yeah, I noticed," Jamie said, meeting Porter's eyes. "That's *why* it was cool. I mean, obviously that guy would've kicked your ass, but you did it anyway."

Porter grimaced. Was it that obvious? He didn't care. Because he had a sneaking suspicion that Jamie was flirting with him. Porter suddenly felt disoriented. What was he doing here sitting with a girl as cute as this? Sitting so close to her he could feel her warmth. Smell her shampoo.

A roar went up somewhere in the bowling alley. It was League Night and the competition was fierce.

Porter thought of something else. Something that had been nagging at him in the back of his mind. He fixed Jamie with his gaze. "Could you have done it?"

"Done what?"

"Beaten Reggie at pool. He's pretty good, you know."

"He's real good," Jamie admitted.

"But you could have beaten him, right?" Porter asked hopefully. The thought of losing all that money on a sucker bet was driving him crazy.

Jamie looked Porter in the eye. "There was no way I could've beaten him."

Porter was stunned. "Get out of here! I—I almost bet a thousand dollars on that game!"

Jamie shrugged. "Hey, I didn't tell you to, you know? No one made you do it."

She had a point there, Porter had to admit.

"I mean . . . it was cool anyway." She shook her head. "Phew. *A thousand dollars.* I didn't know it was that much. You've got balls, Porter."

Porter blushed. "Well . . . thank you." He looked down at his watch to hide his embarrassment and noticed the time. Almost curfew. He looked back at her again. "Well . . . got to get going," he said.

"Why?"

"I have to get back to the academy before curfew," Porter said, reaching for his wallet.

"Curfew?" Jamie asked.

"Yeah, you know," Porter said sheepishly. "That's the way it is at the academy. It's like the army."

"What happens if you don't make it back in time? Do you turn into a pumpkin or something?" Jamie asked, affecting an innocent smile.

"Worse," Porter said. *"Extra guard duty.* It's like a four hour detention."

"What do you guard?"

"Oh . . . I don't know. The wall I guess."

"The wall?"

"There's a stone wall that surrounds the academy. You know, to keep the girls from Cooper Riding Academy from storming our dormitories at night."

Jamie laughed.

Porter pulled a few bills from his wallet, left enough for tab and tip. He knew he had better ask her now before he chickened out. "Er . . . you wanna hook up tomorrow night at the Night Owl?"

"Sure." Jamie grabbed her helmet. "You wanna ride back?"

"If you could drop me off at my car that'd be great."

They boarded the Harley and zipped back to the Night Owl.

Jamie rolled up in front of Porter's car and Porter climbed off. He dug around in his jeans pocket looking for his car keys and thinking of something witty to say before Jamie rode away. But all the awful things that had been happening to him lately had worn him down. He couldn't think straight any more, so he just leaned forward and kissed her. Full on the lips.

She kissed him back.

It was weird kissing a girl wearing a motorcycle helmet straddling an idling motorcycle. He could feel the vibrations go right through her into him.

Or maybe that was just the way she kissed.

Monday afternoon, back on campus, Porter took bets from his usual customers. He expected, almost hoped, that the higher ante would discourage them so he could get out of his partnership with the Jaggers gracefully. And some of his customers did give him the brush off, but the richer ones were more than happy with the higher stakes.

Even subtracting the Jaggers' percentage, Porter was making more money than ever. A lot more.

That night, Porter was in a great mood when he pulled into the parking lot of the Night Owl. He was looking forward to seeing Jamie, and maybe even getting lucky. There was no doubt in his mind she was a passionate girl, and he was more than ready for it.

But Jamie didn't show up at the Night Owl for their date that night.

Porter was incredibly disappointed. It wasn't often a girl took an interest in him. In fact, he could never remember it happening before. *She must've come to her senses,* he realized. She probably found some good-looking jock at Cooper Hollow High to ride on her bike with her. With her looks, she wasn't going to be available for long, Porter sadly admitted to himself. He continued to do business in his booth every night that week, and wait for Jamie, but she never showed up.

Porter found himself returning to the academy each night with a sick, empty feeling.

Yeah, she must have found another guy.

Unless something had happened to her.

Friday night

Porter waited in his booth for the Jaggers. Despite his initial misgivings about their partnership he had to admit it was working out pretty much the way they had said it would. The money was pouring in, the action hotter and heavier than he would have ever imagined.

In fact, in another month or two, at the rate he was going, he'd have enough money to stop altogether. He could always start it up again once he was in college. Without the inhibiting atmosphere of the academy to hinder him, he'd make a ton of money. He might make so much money he'd just forget entirely about Wall Street and become a full-time bookie. Sure, why not? Money was money, what did it matter how you got it?

Porter knew he couldn't keep this up through the end of the school year. The heavier betting action was bound to attract too much attention. He had to get out before Colonel Green, the headmaster of HMA, or Sergeant Saunders, Green's assistant, got wind of his bookie operation. If they ever did, he knew he would be expelled immediately.

Tommy walked into the Night Owl and nodded at Porter. Porter nodded back. Tommy took up his usual place at the bar.

A few minutes later, the Jaggers came in with Booger in tow. They slid into Porter's booth. Skip, as usual, was rattling his dice around in his hand. Porter felt his stomach flutter. Even with Tommy nearby, the Jaggers still made him very nervous. Especially now that he knew they were cold-blooded murderers. He wordlessly slid an envelope full of money over to Skip, who slid it over to Booger, who quickly counted it.

Booger looked over to the Jaggers and nodded. "He doubled our original investment in only one week, Skip," Booger said, giving the envelope to Red, who stuffed it into a large pocket of his army fatigue jacket.

Skip looked at Porter with admiration. "So, what's your system?"

"I don't have a system."

"You must have something. No one can keep picking winners like that on luck."

Porter shrugged. "I get a feeling."

Skip smiled and rolled the dice. It came up an seven—a winner in craps. "I get that feeling myself, sometimes. I call it the *getting rich feeling*. In fact, I'm feeling so good I'm thinking of expanding our little business arrangement."

Porter was skeptical. "I don't think so. I don't think I could squeeze much more out of these guys."

"What about the others?"

"What others?"

"The ones that don't gamble. Maybe there's something else they wouldn't mind spending their money on."

"Like what?" Porter asked, fighting back the uneasy feeling that tightened his stomach muscles.

"Like those four cases of liquor we got stowed in the trunk of our car," Red said with a laugh.

"The four cases of liquor you're going to smuggle into the academy and sell for us," Skip said with a cunning smile.

Nine

Porter shook his head. "I don't think so guys. That's not my game."

"Skip thinks it is," Red said as if that was all there was to it.

"Look guys," Porter pleaded. "This is getting to be a little too much for me. I'm not in your league. I'm just a kid trying to make some pocket money for college. I'm small potatoes. I'm not into smuggling booze and murdering people . . ." Porter realized too late what he had just said.

Skip eyed Porter closely. "You've been checking up on us, twerp? Maybe it's time for a ride. Have you ever seen lover's leap from an upside down position? Dangling over the edge of it with a rope tied to your foot?"

It was now or never. Porter decided to play his trump card. He breathed out heavily. He pointed in the direction of the bar. "See that big guy at the bar taking up two bar stools?"

Skip and Red turned and looked at Tommy who smiled back pleasantly, his big paw scooping a handful of popcorn from the basket sitting on the bartop.

"That guy loves me like a brother. He'd take a bullet for me, he really would. So if you guys want to try any more rough stuff you're going to have to try it on him, first. Only I don't think he'll be as easygoing about it as I was."

Skip looked back at Porter and laughed. "Bringing in the heavy artillery are you, squirt?"

Porter held up his hands. "You forced me into it. Now can we just wish each other good luck and part ways peacefully?" Porter asked hopefully.

"We could, but perhaps you'll reconsider after you've taken a look at this," Skip said as he reached inside his jacket. Porter froze. Skip wouldn't shoot him right here in the Night Owl, would he?

But Skip didn't pull out a gun. It was only a small white envelope which he dropped in front of Porter.

"We'll be waiting for you in the parking lot," Skip said, waving to Red and Booger to slide out of the booth. "You can pick up the booze from our car and transfer it to yours. How you smuggle it into the academy is your problem."

Porter watched them leave before he opened the envelope. There were snapshots of him in the front seat of the T-bird. Behind his head a hand held open his little black book to reveal columns of numbers and initials. Porter's face was in profile, but only the back of the Jaggers heads could be seen, not enough for a positive identification. The hands that held up the code book and took the pictures obviously belonged to Booger. Porter remembered the clicking sounds he heard coming from the back seat the first time the Jaggers snatched him.

Booger the photographer.

The Jaggers were blackmailing him.

Porter doubted if the incriminating evidence would ever stand up in a court of law. Not unless they could crack his code, which he seriously doubted. But he'd have a hard time explaining it to Colonel Green or Sergeant Saunders.

Tommy came over and sat next to Porter. "How'd it go?"

"Not so good."

"You want me to break a few fingers or something?" Tommy asked, popping his knuckles. "I only saw three of them. Two, really. The little guy's a flea."

Porter shook his head. "I need your help with something else. You know that hundred bucks you lost on the Phoenix-Bucks game?"

"Yeah, yeah, I know," Tommy muttered. "I'm a loser—"

"You want to earn it back?"

"Sure. Doing what?" It was typical of Tommy to agree to do something before knowing what it was.

"Smuggling something on base."

The Jaggers had given Porter until the end of the week to get rid of the booze. With Tommy's help, it had taken them only three days. The last bottle had gone when Quincy Tolbert, Reggie Reeves' roommate, had come banging loudly on their door at two in the morning, drunk as a skunk.

Porter handled the sale as quickly as he could, but

the damage had been done. Quincy's late night door banging had awakened half the dormitory floor. Porter knew things couldn't continue like this; his cover was going to get blown in a hurry. It wasn't like at the Night Owl, where the crowds of teenagers who flocked to the club offered a blanket of anonymity.

The academy had many eyes. And some of those eyes had seen Quincy Tolbert stagger drunkenly back to his room after leaving Porter's room. It was bad enough if he got expelled, but it would be even worse if he got Tommy expelled. Tommy loved the academy almost as much as he loved cheerleaders and sports. Porter didn't even want to think about what Tommy might do to him if he got kicked out of the academy on account of him.

He had to end his partnership with the Jaggers and as amicably as possible. Maybe he could buy them out. He didn't like the idea, he never liked to lose money, but he had to be a realist, and in the real world people got killed.

It was worth a try.

And if that didn't work, he still had Tommy.

The following Friday night, Porter found himself sitting at his booth with the Jaggers and Booger. Tommy was sitting at his usual place at the bar, keeping an eye on Porter when he wasn't checking out Jenny Demos' legs.

Porter had offered to buy the Jaggers out for forty thousand dollars—his entire savings—but Skip had laughed right in his face.

"I don't think so, sport," Skip said, rolling his dice.

"That's a lot of dough, but we can make a lot more with the way things are now. And it's just as easy." The dice had come up eleven—another winner at craps.

No kidding. I'm the one taking all the risks.

"In fact," Skip went on, "You did such a good job getting rid of that booze, I've decided to expand our business *even further.* We've got a pound of Mexican brown coming in tomorrow. That's sixteen ounces. Move it at two fifty an ounce. That means . . . er, that would come to . . ." Skip shot a glance at Booger.

"Four thousand dollars, Skip," Booger said.

"That's four thousand dollars you'll owe me at the end of the week. On top of our regular take."

"No way, man," Porter protested. "I'm going to get caught. It's too much of a gamble."

"All life's a gamble, twerp. Now you just do what we tell you or else. You got that, pal?"

Porter had heard enough. He stood up angrily. "I don't think so, *pal!* If you think I'm going to deal—"

"Sit down and shut up!" Skip shouted angrily at Porter as he looked about the room. He glared at Porter and said in a lower voice, "Before you get us all arrested." Red looked disdainfully at Porter and cracked his knuckles loudly. Porter sat back down.

"I'm through playing games with you, soldier boy," Skip snarled, pocketing his dice. "Now you meet us tomorrow night to pick up the weed," he said, the tone of his voice didn't leave any room for argument.

Skip slid out of the booth, followed by his brother and Booger. "I'll let you know later where the drop off spot's going to be. You just make sure you're there on time." The Jaggers and Booger left.

They hadn't even mentioned Porter's cut of the drug money.

Not that he would've taken it.

He had taken about all he was going to take.

Ten

After the Jaggers left, Tommy came over to Porter's booth. "How'd it go?" he asked.

Porter was leaning back in the booth seat staring at the ceiling with bleary eyes. He hadn't slept well the night before. His head felt as heavy as a bowling ball. He focused his attention back on Tommy. "Not so good."

"How do you want me to handle it?"

"Good question," Porter muttered, sitting up. His plan hadn't exactly worked, to say the least. Now, faced with the actual prospect of violence, he grew squeamish. Tommy waited expectantly like a loyal puppy. "Give me a little time to think about it. Okay, big guy?"

"All right, little buddy." Tommy turned to leave but stopped in midstride. "Oh, ah . . ."

Porter reached automatically for his little black book.

"What's the line on the Knicks-Celtics game?" Tommy asked.

"Knicks plus four."

"I'll take the Knicks."

Porter hesitated. The guy never learned. "You sure you want the Knicks?"

"I love the Knicks, man. You know that."

"Yeah, I know. But that doesn't help them beat the spot." Porter shook his head. "It's in Boston Garden. The second game of a home and away. The Knicks just beat the Celtics. They're in the same conference. The Celtics are going to come back with a vengeance on their home court. They've beaten the spot on the home and away *seventy percent* of the time in the past *eight* years. Do you really think that trend's going to change over night? Are you sure you still want the Knicks?"

Tommy nodded. "I just think they can do it, that's all. They're long overdue to win one in Boston Garden."

Porter let out a long sigh. "You're hopeless, man."

"Make it a hundred," Tommy said, before leaving.

Porter wrote the bet down and slipped the black book back into his jacket pocket. He leaned back and stared up at a dark corner of the ceiling covered with cobwebs. He thought for a brief moment he saw a child's face up in the shadows, caught in a spider's web, silently crying. He took his glasses off, wiped them clean, put them back on, and looked up into the shadows. But the face was gone.

Porter didn't know if he were seeing things or not. But he could easily imagine how that kid felt. He felt as if *he* had somehow been caught in that web. The Jaggers were the spider. And they were crawling closer all the time.

He buried his head in his hands.

Life was strange and twisted.

He really needed a vacation.

"Earth to Porter."

Porter looked up.

Jamie's smile lit up the room. She wore a tight yellow silk blouse over a short cotton dress that showed off her long, shapely legs—a real kick in the eye. "Will you marry me?" he asked her.

Jamie laughed. "You think because I let you buy me a burger you can marry me?"

"Two burgers. Deluxe."

"You'll have to do better than that."

"Sorry. I thought it was worth a try."

"Try again."

Porter realized he was so tired he wasn't thinking or talking straight. Maybe he should just shut his mouth. Jamie slid in next to him. Their legs touched, waking Porter up a little.

"Sorry about standing you up last Monday night," Jamie apologized. "My uncle caught me coming in late Sunday night and grounded me. He was pretty steamed because it was a school night. And I guess because I took his stupid motorcycle for a ride without asking his permission. You'd think he'd thank me for fixing it, instead he padlocks it." She shook her head bitterly. "The guy's a real disciplinarian."

"That's probably why your parents have him watching out for you."

"Yeah, well, he's doing a good job."

"How'd you get here?"

"I snuck his car out."

Porter chuckled. "You are really something else," he said and shook his head.

Jamie gave him a sour look. "Well, what was I supposed to do? Sneak out the motorcycle? Then the crap would really hit the fan if he caught me. Do you believe my uncle actually drives a Volkswagen *Beetle*. A cop driving a Volkswagen Beetle," she repeated in disbelief. "Didn't he ever see Steve McQueen in *Bullitt?* You look like death warmed over, by the way."

"Thanks for the compliment," Porter said. "I haven't been getting much sleep lately."

"Why? What's up?"

"You don't want to know."

"Try me."

Porter hesitated, then decided to take the plunge. But where should he start? "That guy at the bar, the night you found me hiding under the table, his name's Skip Jagger. He and his brother, and this kid named Booger, are blackmailing me—"

"Blackmailing you?"

"Yeah."

"Why?"

"Well, you see, I have this little gambling operation that I run out of the Night Owl—"

"You're kidding," Jamie said.

Porter was insulted. "No. I'm not kidding."

"Isn't that against the law?"

Porter snorted. "Look who's talking? A motorcycle *and* a car thief."

"I only borrowed them," Jamie said defensively. "So you run this gambling thing out of here?"

"Yeah. Right here, in fact. From this booth. All my customers are guys I go to school with. You know, kind of keep it in the family, maintain a low profile, stuff like that. The academy's pretty rigid with its rules. If I got caught doing the same thing at Cooper Hollow High I'd probably get a week of detention or something, you know? But if I got caught at the academy, they'd kick me out before I had a chance to pack."

"So why don't you just stop?"

"You should see the money I make," Porter said proudly.

"Yeah, but . . . is it worth the hassle?"

"It was until the Jaggers came along."

"So what happens if you get kicked out of the academy?"

"It would be just like flunking out of school. I'd have to take my entire senior year all over again."

"At Cooper Hollow High?"

"Yeah."

"In other words," Jamie said. "You would be taking your senior year at Cooper Hollow the same year I would. Right?"

The last three years Porter had spent in the stifling academy were for him the longest of his life. He couldn't wait to graduate and get on with his real life. College and girls. And spending his money openly instead of sneaking around so no one would ask him where he got the cash. Once he got into college, he didn't care who knew how much money he had or how he had made it. He didn't know if he wanted to take his senior year over. Even for a girl as cute as Jamie. It just didn't fit into his plans. His course was charted, and he was determined to stay on it.

Besides, she would only dump him in the end.

"Yeah, but then I'd have a hard time getting into college if I got kicked out of the academy."

"I'm sure there's plenty of colleges that would still take you," Jamie reassured him.

"Not Harvard."

"What's so special about Harvard?"

Porter couldn't believe that Jamie was so naive. Graduating from an Ivy League school, especially Harvard, practically guaranteed him a prime spot in the world.

"It's special because—" Porter began counting off his fingers. "Harvard is connections, Harvard is networking, Harvard is the Ivy League, Harvard beats Yale, Harvard is a stepping stone, Harvard is money. Harvard is *big* money." He paused and put down his hand. "And Harvard is . . . out. If I get kicked out of the academy."

"How are they blackmailing you?" Jamie asked.

"They have these incriminating photos of me—"

"Yeah?" Jamie asked enthusiastically. "Like . . . photos of you in bed with the dean's wife or something?"

Porter laughed. "You've obviously never seen Colonel Green's wife."

"Who's Colonel Green?"

"He's the headmaster at HMA. It's like a dean. I've seen his wife a couple of times on campus. She's as fat as Colonel Green is skinny. And she has some kind of disease that makes her eyes bug out."

"Ugh. Sorry I asked. Okay, so let's get back to your criminal activities—" Jamie was really interested, Porter could tell.

"So the Jaggers wanted to back my bookie operation with heavy money in exchange for a cut of the action. But from there it went to bootlegging booze and now they want me to start smuggling in drugs to the academy. It sucks. It's totally out of control!"

"No kidding." Jamie was enthralled.

"Wait, there's more," Porter went on, now that the floodgates had been opened. "I think the Jaggers probably murdered someone—"

"Murdered someone?"

"Yeah. A biker named Barker. Biker as in Hell's Angels-type-biker And his brother—this huge guy named Meat Bomb—has sworn to kill them both with his bare hands . . ."

Jamie broke out into a spasm of giggles. "Sorry," she said, between giggles, when she saw Porter glaring at her. "But, I don't know, it just seems kind of funny to me. Bikers named Meat Bomb and gambling and bootlegging . . . you know, it's like some gangster movie."

But Porter wasn't laughing with her. "It's not funny," he said with quiet seriousness. "And it's not a movie. It's my life."

Jamie was silent for a moment as she studied Porter's face. "I think it's time you went to the police."

"I can't do that."

"Why not?"

"I just told you why. I'd get kicked out of the academy—"

"Hey, Porter," Jamie cut in. "Screw the academy! If these Jagger guys are for real they might kill *you.* Or the other one. The meat guy."

"It's not that simple."

"What's easier than dialling 911?"

"You don't understand." Porter was getting exasperated. "I promised my father I'd graduate from the academy."

"You promised . . . so break your stupid promise!"

"Easy for you to say. I—I made that promise on my father's *death bed.* I told him I'd stick it out at the academy no matter how tough things got—"

"Porter," Jamie broke in. "I don't mean to sound cold, but your father's dead—and you're alive—so why don't we try to keep it that way? Go to the police. You can worry about Harvard and your promises to dead people later."

Dead people? That was his father she was referring to. Porter said nothing.

She just didn't understand. She didn't know what it was like to grow up a nerd, the butt of everyone's jokes. He *had* to graduate from the Hudson Military Academy. He *had* to get into the best college. He *had* to get the best job on Wall Street. He *had* to make the most money. Enough money to jam it right up the noses of all those pompous blue-blooded prick cadets that had everything handed to them all their lives. Life just wasn't as simple as Jamie made it out to be.

"Earth to Porter," she said again, waving her arms in front of his face.

"I'll think about it," he said, tight-lipped.

"Don't think about it, just do it!" Jamie said, mimicking a Nike commercial.

It was easy for her to say. But it was his life. "Yeah, all right," he said, remaining noncommittal.

But she wasn't going to let it go. "So you'll do it?"

"Yeah, yeah, all right. I'll go."

"For real?" Jamie asked.

"For real."

"You promise?"

"I promise."

"When?" she asked suspiciously.

"Tonight. Soon as I leave here."

"No lie?"

"No lie."

Jamie brightened. "See if you can talk to my uncle. He works the night shift. His name is Murphy. Officer Sam Murphy." Porter went through the motions of writing his name down in his little black book.

"Porter," Jamie said, taking his hand. "Don't you ever lie to me. I've had too many boys do that already. For just once in my life I'd like to meet a guy who's different. A guy I can trust. I'm tired of all the losers who say things they don't mean."

"Jamie," Porter said, squeezing her hand, looking her in the eye. "I have never lied to a girl in my life." Which wasn't exactly a lie. He had never had the opportunity before. But having done it, he found it easier than he thought.

Jamie glanced at her watch. "Well, I've got to get back before curfew."

"Before you turn into a pumpkin," Porter joked, not wanting to let go of her hand.

"Before my uncle checks back at the house and finds me missing."

"When will I see you again?" Porter asked anxiously.

"Monday I'm a free girl again," she said.

"Until Monday," Porter said.

She leaned over and kissed him, deep and full, holding it for a long time. Porter just let himself slip into sweet oblivion. He felt her arms encircle him, and he moved his hands up and down her back. She broke the kiss and pressed her warm body against his. He pulled her closer to him and soon the Jaggers were a dim memory. They stayed like that for a long moment until Jamie pulled away.

"Gotta go," she said and gave him a big smile. "See ya."

Porter watched her slide out of the booth and walk away with a sexy swagger—cool and insolent.

And he knew in that instant that he was in love.

He was so entranced that he barely noticed someone a few booths away suddenly get up and leave. He only glimpsed the boy, but he thought it was Booger. Porter suddenly felt in grave danger. If it was Booger, and if he had been spying on Jamie and himself, then he probably heard Porter tell her that he was going to the police. He had no way of knowing it was a lie. If it got back to the Jaggers that he was going to the police, he doubted if he'd make it back to the academy alive.

Porter was about to go after Booger when Tommy came over. Tommy looked at Porter with newfound admiration in his eyes. "Was I hallucinating or did I just see you sucking face with that cute little number I saw in the billiards room last week?"

Porter bristled. "She isn't a number. Her name is Jamie." Unlike Tommy, Porter didn't want to turn his evening with Jamie into a sex story for Tommy's listening pleasure. Besides, he had to find Booger before it was too late. He started to get up from the booth, but Tommy playfully pushed him back in his seat.

Tommy smirked. "Have you been holding out on me, little buddy?"

"Have you ever known me to hold out on you?"

"I've never known you to have a girl. Except some of the skanks I've fixed you up with. So what's the deal with this babe?" Tommy was practically bursting with lust. "Think maybe I could get into some of that?"

Just the thought of Tommy running his big paws all over Jamie, his Jamie, nearly made him sick. "She's not for you."

"Cadets share, little buddy, you know that."

Porter was getting pissed-off. Tommy could have his pick of any girl, why did he have to go after Jamie? The answer was simple. He had seen her with Porter. That was all the reason Tommy needed. And Porter knew that Tommy wouldn't quit until he got into her pants.

"So what do you say, pal? Just a little taste, huh?" Tommy asked lasciviously. "I'll leave enough for you."

The bastard. At that moment, Porter hated Tommy. Hated him enough to do something really cruel to him. And he knew just what to do. "Big guy, sit down, I have a little secret to tell you," Porter said suggestively.

Tommy sat down anxiously, no doubt expecting to hear some wild sex story about Jamie. If he wanted a taste, Porter would give him something to chew on. Porter took a deep breath and gave Tommy a serious look. "Big guy . . . I've been giving it a lot of thought, and I've decided to go to the police."

An uneasy silence followed.

"About the gambling?" Tommy asked. His boisterous mood had evaporated. He was deadly serious.

"About everything."

Tommy just shook his head. "You can't do that, Porter. You'll get us both kicked out of the academy."

Porter tried not to smile. This was easier than he thought. He really had the big lug going. "Don't worry about it, big guy. I'll keep you out of this."

Porter noticed a little vein on Tommy's forehead pulsing with blood. That usually only happened during the last two minutes of a big game. Porter knew he had zapped him good. "I don't see how," Tommy said in a voice that was as cold as ice. "Once the police start grilling you and stuff, you know it's all going to come out. I can't let that happen, little buddy. The academy means too much to me."

It was hard not to goof on Tommy. He was so gullible. And stupid. *The academy means too much to me.* Was he serious or what? Porter gave Tommy's broad neck a little squeeze. "Don't worry about it. I'm taking full responsibility."

Porter could feel the thick cords of muscles in Tommy's neck tighten up. "I don't know, man, I don't know . . ." Tommy suddenly slid out of the booth and quickly disappeared into the crowd.

Porter had a sneaking suspicion he may have pushed the big guy too far. "Tommy!" He had taken it a lot harder than Porter anticipated. "Tommy!" Porter shouted after him. "I was just kidding!"

Porter slid out of the booth and ran after Tommy,

but he had already disappeared into the crowd. He fumbled for his car keys as he hurried to the parking lot. Maybe he had gone back to the academy. He'd better go reassure him. *Just kidding, dude!* There was no way Porter would implicate Tommy. Not if he wanted to live. Not unless he wanted the walls of their room to drip hot blood. His blood. Porter jogged across the parking lot to his car. He yanked open the door and slid in behind the steering wheel, snapped on his seatbelt and rammed the keys into the ignition. The big engine started with a roar. Porter headed the car out of the parking lot and up Thirteen Bends Road.

He hadn't gone far when he felt the cool barrel of a gun press into the skin behind his ear.

Eleven

The voice from the backseat was low and raspy. "Head for town. Or I'll repaint the insides of this car with your brains." The dark figure behind him pushed the gun barrel into the back of Porter's head.

Porter clenched his teeth. "Who are you? What do you want?"

"Your ass," the voice growled.

Porter felt the back of his head drilled with staring eyes.

He affected a cool grin. "You can have it. It's never done me any good."

"How about I rip off your face instead and feed it to the birds you little wiseass!"

Fear trip-hammered Porter's adrenaline. This guy might be a total nut case. His grasp on the steering wheel was cool and sweaty at the same time. He prepared to brake hard and send his assailant flying through the front window if he had to. He slowly applied pressure to the gas pedal. The big Olds picked up speed and shot through the night.

"Don't try anything funny or you'll have a window

where your brain used to be." The figure in the backseat again nudged Porter behind his ear with the gun barrel.

Porter drove in silence for a few moments before he felt the pressure at the back of his head release. Quickly he glanced in the rearview mirror. The dark figure had his cap pulled low over his head and was looking out the back window. Porter prepared to slam on the brakes. Then the head turned back his way, and Porter felt the barrel pressed into the back of his skull again. "Turn right on Old Wilson Highway."

As they approached town, Porter asked, "What's the deal, man? Who are you?"

"The Boogerman," the voice growled. They passed beneath a streetlight and Porter again looked in the rearview mirror. This time he could see Booger's face grinning back at him like a lunatic. "Pull over right here." Porter pulled over. Booger climbed over the front seat with his "gun"—an empty beer bottle. "Had you crapping bricks, didn't I?" Booger asked with a smug smile. Then he giggled as he made himself comfortable in the front seat. "Man, you are so easy!"

Porter was furious. He had no patience for stupid pranks. There was too much at stake for him—like his life. "I almost put you through the front window, you had me fooled so much you moron!"

"Oooh . . . tough guy," Booger teased.

Porter looked over at Booger's skinny body, even skinnier than his own. "You're probably the only guy whose ass I *could* kick. What's with the melodramatics? Do you have tryouts coming up for the Drama Club?"

"I wanted to show you how easy it is to get to you. You don't even lock your car."

"Why should I lock it? There's nothing to steal."

"To keep out guys like me, maybe?"

"Thanks for the advice. So what's your point?"

"I wanted to warn you."

"Warn *me*? I thought you were on their side."

"I'm on my own side now."

"Why? What happened?"

"The same thing that happened to you. I got deeper and deeper into something and didn't know how to get out."

"I would have gotten out if you hadn't taken those pictures!"

Booger got defensive. "You think I wanted to? The Jaggers are sick. I hate those guys."

"So why'd you do it?"

"The same reason you're selling their liquor. They're blackmailing me. They're holding something over my head, too."

"What?"

"It doesn't matter. The only thing that matters right now is that you understand how they operate. They get something on you. They blackmail you. Then they bleed you dry. That's what they've been doing to me, and that's what they're doing to you now."

"Tell me something I don't already know."

"It's going to get worse. And there's no way to reason with those two guys. If you're smart, you'll do what I'm going to do."

"And what's that?"

"Get outta here."

Porter shook his head. "There's got to be another

101

way." Porter couldn't just leave the academy . . . and Jamie.

"There is. But I assumed you wanted to live."

For the first time Porter gave it some serious thought. "If the Jaggers are really that far gone, maybe we should go to the police."

"You've got to be kidding."

"Maybe the two of us could give them enough evidence to make a case against the Jaggers. They couldn't get to us if they were in prison."

"Evidence of what? Gambling? Selling booze to minors. That's not exactly life imprisonment. What happens when they get out? Do you think they're just going to forget about you? Believe me, they won't. I know how these guys operate. They'll hunt you down and kill you."

Porter stared into the black night. He knew Booger was right.

"Drop me off over there," Booger said, interrupting Porter's thoughts.

Porter turned into the Greyhound Station and parked the car. He looked over at Booger. "You're really going to just leave?"

"Yeah. And if you're smart, you'll do the same. Run while your legs are still intact."

"Run where?"

"To New York City. I think I can get something going there."

"Get what going?"

Booger shrugged. "Just . . . something."

"How old are you, Booger?"

"Fifteen."

Porter stared at Booger and saw almost a mirror

image of himself at the same age. He knew what it felt like to be Booger—a nerdy loner looking for a way out; a kid low on self-esteem. He felt sorry for him, but he didn't want to be like him. He dug into his pocket and gave Booger all the money he had. "Well . . . hang in there, little buddy. And good luck."

Booger quickly took the money, as if he thought Porter would change his mind. "Thanks, man. Thanks a lot. That's pretty damn decent of you, man, considering, you know, I took those pictures and all. You probably wouldn't be in this jam now if it wasn't for me."

Porter shrugged. "Forget about it. If it hadn't been you, it would've been someone else."

Booger glanced at his watch. "I've got a couple of hours to kill before the bus to New York gets here." He gave Porter a sly smile. "And a couple of fake IDs. You want to go for a few beers?"

Porter looked at Booger's anxious, pimply face. "No. I've got to get back to the academy. But thanks anyway."

"Okay, bro." Booger held out his hand and Porter slapped it. "I owe you one."

Booger walked into the tiny Greyhound Station to buy his bus ticket. Porter turned the car around and headed back to the academy to find Tommy.

Porter slipped his key into the lock and entered his room. He had expected to find Tommy either in the weight room or pacing around their room trying to vent his anger. But he was surprised to find that Tommy had already nodded off and was snoring away.

Porter decided to let Tommy sleep.

Porter had had all sorts of gruesome images on the drive to the academy. Mostly all the things Tommy might do to him if he didn't change his mind about going to the police. He quietly undressed by his nightlight and slipped into his terry cloth robe and flip-flops. He grabbed his soap and room key, left the room, and padded down to the communal showers. He hit the spray and turned up the heat. The shower room quickly filled with steam.

The hot water felt great. As if it could get into his pores and wash away all the hassles away. Hassles. God. It didn't seem fair. Why him? At least he had one good thing happen to him. He had met Jamie. He wished she were there in the shower with him right now.

The lights went out.

"Listen up, asshole!" came a voice out of the darkness. The hot water pounded down on Porter. But still he felt a chill. "Meet the Jaggers tomorrow," a voice echoed through the darkness. "Or your little girl friend's going to get messed up."

Twelve

Porter hunkered down in the open shower stall. He felt incredibly vulnerable in the dark shower room as the water pelted down upon his naked body. He hunched rigidly and listened for the sound of any movement. Of anyone coming his way. The shower water continued to splatter down on the tiled floor of the shower stall. That was all he heard. That and the sound of his own beating heart. He quickly rinsed off and threw his robe on, slipped on his flip flops, and crept back to his room. He unlocked the door, entered the dark room, closed the door, turned and knocked into something big and solid.

Porter's scream was cut off when a hand shot out and gripped his neck in a strangle hold.

The lights went on. Tommy was holding Porter tightly around the neck with one big meaty hand, the other hand was still on the light switch. He seemed surprised that it was Porter.

"Lay off, you goof," Porter rasped, pulling back on one of Tommy's massive fingers.

Tommy let go of Porter's neck. "I thought you were someone else."

The color slowly returned to Porter's face as he rubbed his neck. "Who else would be coming into our room in the middle of the night?"

Tommy opened the door and looked up and down the hallway before poking his head back into the room. "I don't know but someone was trying. Did you see anyone out there?"

"No. But there was someone in the shower room with me."

"Huh?" Tommy gave Porter a funny look. He closed the door and went over to the window, looked out.

Porter told Tommy about the warning in the shower.

"You mean that girl you were French kissing in the Night Owl?"

"Yeah. Jamie. The Jaggers must have a spy here at the academy."

Tommy looked away from the window and at Porter. "No kidding. They've got *you*."

"Besides me."

"Whoever he is, I'm going to beat the crap out of him when I catch him. He was messing around outside our door. Woke me up from a damn fine dream I was having." He looked back out the window.

"See anything?" Porter asked.

"I thought I saw someone running across the lawn before."

"Did you get a good look at him?"

Tommy shrugged. "Not really. But it looked like that kid that was with the Jaggers."

"You mean Booger?" Porter asked in disbelief.

"Whatever his name is. The skinny little kid that was with you guys in the booth tonight. The one with the zits."

"Booger." Porter sat down on the edge of his bed. "Nah, it couldn't be him. I just took him to the Greyhound Station."

"Who?"

"Who are we talking about?"

"You just took this kid Booger to the Greyhound Station?"

"He was running away to New York. He'd had enough of the Jaggers and wanted out."

Tommy started to get dressed.

"Where're you going?"

"I was going to go check with the guard anyway, before you came in. Maybe they caught this Booger punk trying to get back over the wall. If they did, I might have to assist in the interrogation," Tommy said in a cold, humorless voice. Porter wouldn't want to be in Booger's shoes if Tommy were doing the interrogating.

But he didn't think it was Booger. "Hey, dummy. I told you, I just took him to the bus station."

"Did you see him get on the bus?"

"No."

Tommy zipped up his uniform trousers and pulled on his sneakers. "Be right back," he said, slipping out the door.

Porter could hear him jogging down the hallway. Then he noticed something on the floor. A small envelope. He picked up the envelope and tore it open. Inside was a crudely drawn map of the woods that

107

stretched out behind the Night Owl. Marked on the map, a short distance from the Night Owl, was a small trail that lead to a clearing. A typewritten note instructed Porter to meet the Jaggers there tomorrow night at eight o'clock.

Porter tried to make sense of it all. Had Booger left the note? Had that been Booger in the shower? Why would Booger first warn him about the Jaggers then try to scare him into meeting them?

Porter read the note again searching for the angle.

Booger's story about running away could have been a lie—part of a big scam to frighten Porter into cooperating with the Jaggers. After all, what did Porter really know about the Jaggers? Only what Tommy and Booger had told him. He had no proof that they had killed anyone. Tommy could have been fed a lot of bull about the Jaggers just like Booger had fed it to him. It could all be a big hustle.

The door opened and Tommy walked in. "I bumped into the guard in the hallway."

"Did they catch the guy?"

"No. But they saw him run out of this wing. And he fits the description of this Booger creep. What was he wearing when you dropped him off at the Greyhound Station?"

"Ah . . . a Red Devils cap and school jacket."

Tommy nodded an affirmation. "It was him all right. The guards think he went back over the wall. What's that you got in your hand?"

"It's a note from the Jaggers." Porter handed the note to Tommy.

Tommy read the note with a furrowed brow. "Your friend Booger must've left this."

"Sometimes you amaze me with your brilliance, big guy," Porter said, taking back the note.

Tommy ignored Porter's sarcastic put-down, as he always did. "Why do they want to meet you in the woods?"

Porter started to get a plan. "I think they want to unload a pound of dope. You know, have us smuggle it in here and deal it like the booze."

"Isn't dealing drugs to minors in a school zone a violation of the *federal* law?"

Porter was impressed. For a stupid jock, Tommy sure knew his drug laws.

"That's right, Einstein. And if they got caught they'd go up the river forever. They'd be old men before they ever saw the light of day again."

"That's why they want us to do it. So it can't be pinned on them."

"Again, you dazzle me with your perception."

"So what should we do?"

Porter held up his hands as if the solution were the most obvious thing in the world. "We'll pin it on them. Do you still have that little tape recorder you used to carry around with you?" Tommy would sometimes hide a tiny tape recorder beneath his clothing when he went out on dates and then try to get girls to talk dirty to him. Later he'd play the whole conversation back to Porter for a few laughs. Porter was amazed at what Tommy could get a girl to say."

Tommy smiled sheepishly. "Sure. I think it's still in my car."

"Good, get it. I'll need it tomorrow night."

"Wait a minute. You plan on taking this to the police?"

Porter gave Tommy a reassuring smile. "Of course not, big guy. I was just yanking you around. I never had any intention of going to the police." Not unless he had to. "This is just to protect ourselves and get those creeps off our backs."

Tommy seemed relieved as he went to get the tape recorder.

Saturday night

Porter patted his inside jacket pocket to make sure the tape recorder was securely in place. All he had to do was remember to turn the damn thing on at the right time. He reached inside his jacket a few times to make sure he could find the record button without having to take the recorder out of his pocket. He didn't want to hit the play button by mistake. He didn't think the Jaggers would be interested in hearing one of Tommy's old sex tapes.

But then again, maybe they would. He had. Some of those conversations were better than the letters he had read in Tommy's *Penthouse* magazines he kept hidden in the bedsprings of his bunk.

It would be easy. Just get the Jaggers to talk about dealing drugs and record it. Then blackmail them into leaving him alone. Fight fire with fire.

Only Porter wasn't feeling very confident. He had planned to have Tommy go to the meeting place ahead of time with a gun and hide. Just in case something went wrong—such as the Jaggers trying to kill

110

him. But Tommy told him he had pulled extra guard duty for accumulated demerits, so Porter was on his own. And scared witless.

Nah they wouldn't kill me, Porter tried to reassure himself. *What was the angle?*

Porter nervously hurried down the leaf-strewn path that was illuminated by the glow of the moon. He looked up into the sky and saw the full moon like a big yellow cyclops eye staring back down at him.

A full, luminous moon.

Things had gotten totally out of hand. There was absolutely no way he was going to deal dope for the Jaggers, they could just forget about that. He had to make that clear from the start. He didn't even drink beer or smoke cigarettes much less take drugs, and he wasn't about to start dealing them. He had tried smoking pot exactly one time. After a ten minute coughing jag he had made it his last time. Gambling was his buzz. Fleecing the suckers was his high.

Porter knew if he starting selling pot at the academy, it would be just a matter of time before the Jaggers wanted him to start dealing coke. Then what? Crack? Crystal meth? Heroin? No, he just couldn't do it. He would just have to take his chances and hope the Jaggers didn't hurt him too badly.

He didn't think they'd really kill him. It was just a threat, a bluff. He hoped. Oh sure, they had hog-tied him behind the shooting range and left him there to be blasted to bits the next morning. Still, the more he thought about it, the more Porter was convinced that they had just been toying with him. They had probably just been waiting for him to crack. After he had sweated bullets for a while, they would've come back and set him free. *Change your mind yet, twerp?*

Sure, that's what they had done. The Jaggers were just townie punks, not murderers. They were sadistic, not cold-blooded.

He could kick himself for being such a dunce. Such an easy mark. That was his game, doing a number on the suckers. He had let them do a number on him. And Booger was part of it.

It was all part of the hustle.

But that was before he had time to analyze the situation properly, deliberately, like the odds on a gambling spread sheet.

But where was the angle?

There wasn't any. They didn't have one. There was no reason for the Jaggers to kill him.

Unless they knew he was going to the police.

But how could they know that? Unless Booger had told them. The more he thought about it, the more he believed that it wasn't Booger in the shower. Booger had hauled ass. He knew where Booger was coming from. Hell, Porter *was* Booger a few years ago. A scrawny nerd looking for a way out. And the Jaggers knew how to take advantage of people like Booger.

Maybe it was Reggie. Maybe the Jaggers had gotten something on Reggie and were using him to spy on Porter. Hell, Reggie hated him enough to probably do it for nothing. It was their style. Get someone else to do the dirty work while they sat back, spending his money on booze and pot. He could see all that now.

Well chumps, I've got news for you—you can't hustle a hustler.

Porter swallowed hard, trying to deny how petrified he felt. But his heart was beating violently inside his chest.

I should've brought the gun myself, he thought desperately. Except guns scared the hell out of him. Another reason he knew he wasn't exactly cut out for the military life.

The closer he got to the meeting place, the more he regretted that Tommy hadn't come along with him. That guy had more muscles in his pinkie than Porter had in his entire body.

Porter felt like a sitting duck. Every instinct told him not to move another inch. He turned around and walked back the way he had come.

"I'm no damn Rambo," he muttered to himself.

Then Porter heard a voice inside his head. The voice from the shower room. The voice that had spoken to him last night.

"Don't go to the police tomorrow . . . or your little girlfriend's going to get messed up."

He had finally met a girl he cared about, who cared about him, and somehow she had become a pawn in this wicked game. What exactly did that mean, anyway? He shuddered to think of the answer.

He stopped.

Got to go through with it, got to do it. Just go and get it over with. Porter turned back and continued toward the spot where he was supposed to meet the Jaggers. Just go ahead and get it over with. Take it like the man you've never been. Do it for Jamie if not for yourself. Do something right for once in your life—he heard voices.

He stopped dead in his tracks. Fear was hammering adrenalin through his system.

He heard another voice.

And . . . moaning. And sobbing.

Porter quietly snuck up on the clearing and hid behind a thick clump of bushes. He saw Skip Jagger. With a pistol in his hand. Skip looked his way. A demented, shining gaze.

Porter ducked down, his breath catching in his throat. He reached into his denim jacket and with a trembling hand turned the tape recorder on.

"This is what we do to little rats who double-cross us," Porter heard Skip snarl to someone.

"Noo!" someone protested.

Porter, his limbs nearly paralyzed with fear, rose up on his haunches and peeked over the top of the bushes.

It was Booger.

His neck was in a noose and his hands were tied behind his back. The rope was tied from a tree branch. Booger had to stand on his tiptoes or the weight of his body would cause the noose to tighten around his neck and strangle him.

Skip had a pistol stuck in his face.

"No, Skip, please," Booger begged.

Skip pulled back the hammer of the gun until it clicked and locked into place.

"I swear, I never warned Porter. Honest—" Porter saw Booger press his eyes shut as Skip placed the opening of the gun barrel directly on Booger's pimply forehead.

The rest seemed to happen in slow motion.

Skip squeezed the trigger. A shot rang out, flushing a covey of birds from a nearby tree. Porter's mouth dropped open in horror as bits of brain and skull blew out the back of Booger's head.

Porter fell back, as if it *he* had been shot, and stared at the dark sky. At the full moon. He rolled over on all fours and swallowed back vomit.

My god! Skip just killed Booger!

Thirteen

He had seen it with his own two eyes. He was a witness to murder. The reality of it was almost too much for him to comprehend. The overwhelming terror he felt was suffocating him. It gripped him around his chest like a giant vise and threatened to squeeze the sanity out of him.

He could still smell the gunsmoke in the air, still hear the echo of the gunshot reverberating in the chilly night air. The covey of birds flushed from the trees still flew blindly in panic induced angles.

Porter climbed to his feet. His knees felt too weak to support his body. He felt light-headed, sick, but he knew he had to get out of there. He took a step backward and heard a twig snap. He heard a surprised curse from the clearing. Heavy footsteps came his way.

A voice inside Porter shrieked for him to get it together and run. Run! Run for his life. He fought back his nausea and turned away from the approaching footsteps. Then he bolted blindly into the woods. His momentum sent him crashing head first into a hawthorn bush. The thorns slashed at his cheeks as he went down in a heap. He felt as if his face had landed on a porcupine. Only his glasses saved him from being blinded.

The pain of ripped facial skin sent a wake-up call to Porter's frenzied brain. He scrambled to his feet and ran back to the path that led out of the woods and to the Night Owl. This was no time to panic. He had to get to a phone and tell the cops.

Skip came crashing through some honeysuckle bushes and leveled the gun at Porter. "I've got you now, you little punk!"

Porter's reply was to take a slight detour away from Skip and through the woods. He hurdled a gully like a frightened deer and ran back to the main path.

Skip yelled something, but Porter wasn't about to answer him. He hit the main trail and bolted down the leaf strewn path, his arms and legs churning. His lungs were close to bursting, his heart slamming into his ribs. He glanced over his shoulder to see if Skip had followed him.

Skip was running like a madman speed freak with his smoking pistol held high in the air. He slowed only long enough to get off a shot at Porter.

Porter flinched as the gun barrel spat fire, expecting a searing pain to rip through his leg or worse. But the bullet missed him. He turned and kept running until the Night Owl came into view. His lungs were begging for relief. He felt as if someone had slipped a butcher knife between his ribs and was trying to pry out his breathing apparatus. He quickly glanced behind him.

Skip was coming. He was red in the face and gasping for air, but he wasn't slowing down. It must be the speed, Porter thought, the speed coursing through Skip's body was giving him stamina he didn't normally possess. All Porter had to match it with was pure adrenalin pumping through his system. And he was almost out of that.

As Porter watched, Skip squeezed off another shot.

The gun barked flame and Porter turned and ran. He made it to the Night Owl and flung open a seldom used side door, ripping off its rusted lock in the process. He took several steps down the hallway before his body gave out. His legs had turned to rubber and just wouldn't work anymore.

He started to crawl. There was a large room at the end of the hallway. He might find help there. He crawled halfway down the hallway before giving up on that as well. He lay on the floor sucking air in large hungry gasps. He thought his chest was going to split wide open. He knew he had to get up. He had to get to a phone and call 911 or scream for help or something.

Skip came skidding through the doorway.

He saw Porter laying in the hallway and slowed to a walk. Then he knelt down beside Porter and stuck the gun barrel behind his ear and pulled back the trigger.

Porter lowered his head, squeezed his eyes shut, and waited for death to greet him.

Fourteen

Porter wondered how long it would take to die and took a deep breath. He listened for the bullet, but heard footsteps instead. He knew Skip would kill any witness to his grisly brutality. He tried to yell a warning but had no breath for it. He raised his head and looked up the hallway. Everything was in a haze, a blur. Through the mist he saw two very bright violet eyes staring back at him.

"Run . . ." Porter managed to gasp.

Skip stood up with a sadistic smile on his face. He aimed his gun at the eyes. Then suddenly the hand that held the gun violently jerked back as if yanked by an invisible string. The gun flew through the air behind Skip and clattered harmlessly to the floor. Skip held his arm in disbelief. The air between Skip and the still open door at the end of the hallway came alive as if invaded by a horde of invisible bumble bees. A hungry wind sucked Skip backward. He fought to stay on his feet, but he slid back down the hallway with increasing speed until he was pulled out the door with an audible pop!

Then the door banged shut like a rifle shot. Porter had watched it all, bewildered.

And then he passed out.

Porter felt a hard slap and opened his eyes. He stared up into the face of Reggie Reeves. He sat up and leaned against the wall. His face hurt like hell, but it wasn't from Reggie's slap.

Reggie looked down at him with his usual contemptuous sneer. "If you want to sleep off a drunk, why don't you do it back on campus, Smith? You're gonna tarnish the image of the academy lying around in hallways."

Porter tried to shake the cobwebs out of his head. He looked at his watch, but it must have stopped hours ago. "What time is it?"

"It's time for all good soldier boys to be tucked in bed. We've got twenty minutes to beat curfew. If you weren't a cadet, I would've left you there to rot," Reggie said.

"Yeah, right," Porter replied. "You're a regular Mr. Nice Guy."

"Anyway, as long as I've got your attention, what's the spread on the Duke-North Carolina game?"

"I don't know," Porter said, gingerly touching the scratch marks on his face.

"You don't know?" Reggie asked incredulously. "It's the conference final. Did what ever happen to your face affect your brain as well?"

"Hey Reggie? Shut up, all right? Make your bets with someone else. I'm sick of you. Try the Jaggers. You already work for them anyway."

"Who?"

"Don't act stupid when it comes so naturally." Porter stood up on rubbery legs and almost fell down again.

"You disgusting little peon amateur drinker twit. Don't drink if you can't hold it. You'll give serious drinkers like myself a bad name." Reggie spun on his heel and walked away from Porter.

Porter imagined this must be what it feels like to go through a bad trip. The last hour or two had seemed like one big hallucination to him. The murder, the mad scramble through the woods, kissing his life goodbye, watching Skip get sucked out the door, the door slamming shut by itself.

Was it real or what?

He walked gingerly down the hallway on aching leg muscles until he found a pay phone next to the men's room. He had never run so hard in all his life. How the jocks could do stuff like this everyday was a mystery to him, he'd be sore for a week. The pay phone was being used so he slipped into the men's room to clean up. He studied himself in the mirror and saw what a mess he was. His denim jacket was covered with mud and thorns and his face was dappled red with coagulating blood.

He carefully washed the blood off his face. He dabbed at his scratches with a paper towel and looked at himself in the mirror. His face looked like something the cat dragged in. Well, if anyone said anything about it, he'd make a joke of it and say he'd had a hot date. He wiped his jacket off as best he could and removed as many thorns as he could find. He walked out of the men's room and to the now

121

unoccupied phone. He looked around, saw no one, yanked the phone off the cradle and punched in 911. The police operator immediately came on.

"Nine-one-one. Sergeant Futrynzski."

"I, ah . . . heard some gunshots in the woods," Porter blurted out.

"Where did this happen, sir?"

"Behind the Night Owl Club. I was walking on the trail behind the Night Owl and heard what I thought were some gunshots. It's on the trail that joins the club to the Hudson Military Academy. Closer to the club. Maybe a half mile or so. You'll see a fallen pine tree. Take the small trail to a clearing. Sounded like it came from the clearing. I guess it could've been firecrackers." Porter realized he was babbling so he hung up. They had enough to go on.

Enough to find Booger's body.

Porter patted his jacket pocket, an old habit, to make sure his little black book hadn't fallen out. He patted something else, too—the tape recorder. He had completely forgotten about it. He'd have to check it out back at the academy to see if Skip and Booger's voices had come through. He might have the goods on Skip after all.

Porter ran across the parking lot to his car, took a quick glance in the backseat to make sure he had no unwanted hitchhikers, and jumped in. He jammed his key into the ignition and cranked the motor over. He burned rubber as he shot out of the parking lot and nearly lost control of the car at the exit. He slowed down and made his way onto Thirteen Bends Road.

He slid his window down and let the cold night

air wash over him, reviving him. He breathed deeply to calm himself. This was a very dangerous road. Many teenagers had died because they drove carelessly on its winding curves.

Suddenly, Porter's car was rammed from behind with a vicious jolt, snapping back his head, nearly giving him whiplash. He shot a fearful glance in his rearview mirror and saw a car behind him with its lights off. He directed his attention back to the road—too late. He had missed a turn as the road suddenly dipped and turned and his big Olds slammed into a guardrail. Porter fought to control the car as it slid back onto the road then again into the guardrail. The front of the car was sprayed with sparks as metal rubbed metal. Porter jerked the steering wheel hard to the left to get off the rail. The back end swung around, and the Olds shot backward for a few frightening moments.

Long enough for Porter to see the Jaggers in their black Thunderbird pull to a stop on the shoulder of the road to watch the show.

The tires of the Olds shuddered and screeched as the car went into a sideways slide. It hit the guardrail again at an odd angle and went airborne. The car jumped the rail and plummeted front end first down a steep incline where it rolled into a small ravine and flipped. It rolled twice more before landing upside down.

Then the car burst into flames.

Fifteen

The black Thunderbird pulled up alongside the guardrail where Porter's car had flipped out. Skip bolted out of the driver's side with his gun drawn and hurdled the guardrail. There was a reason for the guardrail, as Skip soon discovered, when he went headfirst down the steep incline. He lost his gun as he slid on his nose halfway down the incline. He crawled to this feet cursing angrily, picking bits of gravel out of his elbows and knees. He looked around for his gun.

Smoke was pouring out of Porter's car, flames licking out of the shattered back window.

Skip watched the car burn as if hypnotized by the flames. Then he saw his gun glinting in the moonlight and scooped it up. With a little more caution this time, he made his way down the incline, to the ravine, where the car lay burning.

Red appeared at the guardrail. "Skip! C'mon, there's a car coming up the hill!"

"I'm not finished with that little punk yet!"

"We don't have time for that! Let's get the hell out of here! He's going to fry anyway!"

Skip stared angrily at the car, still about thirty yards down the ravine, and pumped a few shots at it just for the hell of it before scrambling back up the hill.

Porter peeked out from behind a clump of bushes. He had crawled out of the smoking car just in time to see Skip sliding down the hill face-first—a beautiful sight watching that creep's skin peel away as he did his human sled impersonation.

He watched as Skip scrambled back up the hill and disappeared over the guardrail. Porter heard a squeal of tires as the Thunderbird rocketed away. He started to make his way back up the incline but was knocked on his butt when the car suddenly exploded into a big red and orange fireball. The hot wave of the blast swept over him, taking the chill out of the night air and his bones. Porter watched the big car burn and gave silent thanks he hadn't bought one of those little foreign models.

It wasn't until he started climbing up the incline that he realized how badly his ankle hurt. And his head, too. He could already feel a lump growing on it. He recalled dimly that his head had hit either the windshield or the steering wheel when the car flipped. Man, did it hurt. And pain like white heat shot through his ankle every time he put weight on it. Fortunately his shoulder harness and the car's big tank-like frame had protected him from worse injury. And Porter knew it could have been much worse. He was lucky to be alive.

Still, he was going to be some kind of sore in the morning.

At the top of the incline, he was met with the concerned face of an elderly lady who stood by the guardrail looking down at him. Her station wagon was idling on the shoulder of the road with the lights still on.

"Are you all right?" she asked anxiously.

"Yes, ma'am," Porter said as he took the last painful step to reach the top of the incline. He sat down on the guardrail to catch his breath and looked back at his burning hulk of a car.

"I saw that ball of fire come out of the sky like there was a volcano exploding down there. I hope to God there was no one else in that car."

"No, ma'am," Porter said, shaking his head wearily.

"Are you sure you're not hurt? Perhaps I should take you to the hospital. You might be in shock and not even know it."

After tonight, Porter doubted if much of anything would ever shock him again. He politely declined the old woman's request. A hospital meant more questions than Porter cared to answer at the moment. Probably the police, too. Instead he asked the woman if she would drop him off at the academy. It was only after Porter assured her they had an excellent medical facility at the academy that she finally agreed to take him there instead of to a hospital.

Porter climbed into her car, easing his rapidly swelling ankle in after him. The inside of the car was clean and spotless It would have passed the most rigid academy inspection for tidiness, Porter noted, and felt bad about dirtying it up. He was covered with thorns, mud, gravel; he looked in her sideview mirror and saw that his scratched up face was now also covered in black soot from the smoking car. He was surprised that the lady hadn't turned and ran when she saw him coming back up the hill.

She dropped him off at the academy. Porter thanked her and waved goodbye. He waited until her car disappeared before limping up the main drive and into the woods, making a wide detour of the main gate as he made his way to the west wall. The west wall was shielded from the main building and the guard shack by a stand of old oak trees.

Porter had never climbed the wall before and didn't look forward to doing it now. But he had little choice. He had to make it back to his room and get cleaned up. And he had better get his story straight. If he got caught looking the way he did, he'd have an awful lot of explaining to do. The last thing he wanted was to be interrogated by Sergeant Saunders.

Saunders was a burly retired Green Beret who had done three tours of duty in Vietnam. He said it was the most fun he had ever had in his life outside of terrorizing freshmen cadets.

A story circulated around the academy with each incoming wave of plebes that Saunders' specialty in Vietnam was torturing the Cong. It was rumored that he slit off their ears with a razor and made them into a necklace. He would show this grisly little prize to only his favorite cadets. Porter had, for the most part, managed to avoid the sarge since coming to the academy.

And he hoped to keep it that way.

He limped up to the west wall and looked it over.

He guessed it was about seven feet high. He took a running start and jumped as high as he could. He couldn't get much height on his jump because of his twisted ankle, and his fingertips fell woefully short of the top of the wall. Worse, he fell back to the ground on his bad ankle.

He shrieked in pain, his scream shattering the stillness of the night.

Porter thought he might pass out from the agony. He lay flat on the ground and waited for the fire to go out of his ankle. He figured he'd be lucky if he could even stand up. He lay on his back staring up at a million twinkling stars and listened to the crickets. There wasn't much else he could do. He wished he could just close his eyes and go to sleep right there. He might have to if he didn't make it over that wall. Then he heard footsteps running his way and struggled to his feet.

"Halt!" bellowed the guard, running toward him in a loping gait and carrying his mock M-1 rifle chest-high. "Stay right where you are!"

Sixteen

Sunday morning

The guard filled out his report and Porter was returned to his room. He stayed in bed all Sunday, letting his ankle heal up a little along with the rest of his assorted bumps and bruises, getting out of bed only to use the latrine.

He played back the tape recording of Booger's murder.

He was, as he had feared, too far away to pick up anything. He flipped the tape over and stowed the recorder in his locker.

Maybe some other time.

Monday morning

Porter woke up to Tommy's snoring and was afraid to move. He knew his body would still hurt, but he wouldn't know exactly how much until he moved, and he wasn't anxious to find that out. He would've stayed in bed longer except that he had to go to the bathroom. He looked at his clock on the nightstand. He had to get up anyway, it was only twenty minutes until his first class. He gingerly swung his legs out of bed. The nerve ends in his body still painfully protested.

Porter slipped on his flip-flops. The right foot wouldn't go all the way in because of a heavy bandage wrapped around his ankle. He stood and put a little weight on it. Not bad.

Unfortunately the rest of his body felt like a giant, freshly peeled scab.

Porter put a little more pressure on the ankle and felt only a hint of pain. He unraveled the wrap and slowly wiggled his toes. Not too bad at all. Porter slipped his right foot into his flip-flop, threw on his light blue academy bathrobe and made his way out the door and rapidly down the hallway to the bathroom. He really had to go! He made it as far as the latrine door.

"Halt, dumbhead!"

Porter jumped at the scream. Out of the corner of his eye, the burly form of Sergeant Saunders came marching his way. He snapped to attention.

"At ease, dumbhead." Sergeant Saunders called all the cadets dumbhead so Porter didn't take it personally. Saunders stood in front of him with a lit cigar clenched between his teeth and regarded Porter critically with his droopy, blue eyes beneath bushy eyebrows. "Out a little late Saturday night weren't we, dumbhead?"

"Yes, sir." Porter watched the brightly glowing ash from Saunders' cigar bounce perilously close to his right cornea. He had never seen Sergeant Saunders without a cigar stuck in his mouth. He didn't know which to be the most concerned about: wetting his bathrobe or watching the cigar burn a hole in his eyeball.

"That's something I would expect of that dumb jock roommate of yours. Did he put you up to it? Did he have you out all night partying then desert you when the going got tough?"

"No, sir."

"Talk straight to me, dumbhead. And stand at attention. Why are you fidgeting around like that?"

"Sorry sir. I was in a hurry to make it to my first class."

Saunders looked at his watch. "Fifteen minutes, plenty of time. That gives you at least three minutes to do your business, get dressed, and report to me in my office for a little question and answer session. Three minutes. Understood?"

"Yes, sir!"

"Carry on."

Sergeant Saunders did an about-face and marched back down the hallway as Porter hurriedly limped to the latrine.

Five minutes later, Porter was standing at attention and finishing his story in front of Sergeant Saunders' plain wooden desk in his small, unpretentious office. He had made something up about getting into a fight with three kids from Cooper Hollow High who had insulted him and the academy. It was the type of story he thought Saunders might enjoy hearing.

"So after they disparaged the integrity of our fine

institution, I had no recourse but to put them in their place."

"Kicked their asses did you, Smith?" A bright smile lit up Saunders face. He leaned back in his swivel chair and took a leisurely puff on his cigar and blew a long stream of blue smoke at the ceiling. Porter could tell he was enjoying the story—even if he didn't believe it. "Only three of them?"

"Just three, sir. But they were big."

"Too bad. If it had been four or more I might have let you slide on the demerits. But only three? Well, after all, you are an academy man and should be able to handle only three civvies." He paused to tap some ash off the tip of his cigar. "Where'd you fight them, by the way? Inside a chimney? The guard reported they caught you in black face. Or was that so you could sneak back onto the grounds without detection? Is that what it was, Smith? Camouflage? Practicing night time commando tactics for when you join the CIA?"

"No sir. I had a minor car accident. I was in a hurry to get back to the academy before curfew after teaching those punks a lesson. Ah . . . you may have noted on my record that I've never missed curfew before last night, sir."

Saunders had Porter's records open on his desk, but he wasn't looking at them. "Did you report this *minor* accident?"

A long pause. "No sir."

"Why not? A responsible cadet would have reported a car accident right away."

"Ah . . . I was in shock, sir." Porter told the flimsy lie with as much sincerity as he could muster.

Saunders barked out a laugh. "You're full of it, Smith," he said and laughed again. "What's really going on, dumbhead? Talk to the old sarge," he said, sitting up straight in his chair. "I've been hearing some funny rumors around the old academy about you."

Porter said nothing. Booger's murder was still fresh in his mind, and he knew it could easily still happen to him if he said the wrong thing.

Saunders pulled open a drawer on his battered gray desk. He withdrew a small, rectangular piece of plastic and slid it across the desk to Porter. "One of the cadets found that on the grounds and turned it into me yesterday. I thought maybe you could tell me who it belonged to."

Porter glanced at the piece of plastic. It was his Gold American Express card. With his name on it. "Yes sir. I believe that belongs to me."

"Oh," Saunders said, pretending to be surprised. "I saw your name on it, but I thought it must belong to another Porter Smith in Cooper Hollow. I mean, how's a scholarship kid get a Gold Card?"

"Ah . . . it was a gift, sir. From a rich aunt."

"Bull. I know you're up to something, Smith. Come clean with the old sarge. For your own good."

But Porter remained silent.

"Nothing?" Saunders asked.

"No, sir," Porter said in a soft voice.

Saunders shook his head sadly. "How's that ankle of yours, Smith?" he asked sympathetically. "No serious damage done, I hope."

"No, sir. It's fine, sir. Much better."

"Good. Take the four-to-eight watch tonight. Dismissed."

"Yes, sir," Porter said. He sighed with relief and did an about-face, preparing to leave the sergeant's office.

"And Smith?"

Porter did another about-face. "Yes, sir?"

Saunders was holding up his credit card. "Don't forget this."

Monday evening.

Porter stood inside the guard shack near the main entrance of the Hudson Military Academy twirling the dial of the radio. He had come directly to guard duty after his last class, and he was dying to hear some news about Booger's murder. He had been on duty for over an hour and had heard not one word of it on the all news station. Hadn't the police found the body yet? Maybe his directions had been lousy. Thinking back on it, he couldn't even remember what he had told the 911 operator. Perhaps he had been incoherent and hadn't made any sense.

He looked through the little guard shack window and saw Tommy jogging toward him with his gym bag under his arm. He stopped when he reached the guard shack and poked his head in.

"Damn, Porter," Tommy laughed. "I've been going over that wall for almost three years now and never got caught, and you do it once and wind up in Saunders office—what the hell happened to your face?"

Porter grimaced. He had been asked that question all day long and was tired of thinking up inventive answers. "Hot date, " he said, giving Tommy a big wink.

Tommy chortled. "With that hot little honey I saw you with the other night?"

"Yeah. Ms. Beeswax herself."

Tommy scrutinized the large, nasty bruise on Porter's forehead. "God . . . she must play rough."

"That's right. One look at my bod is enough to drive the girls crazy."

Tommy grinned. "For real. What the hell happened to you?" Porter looked over Tommy's shoulder and saw the plebe guard under his command double-timing his way with his mock M-1 rifle held breast-high. The cadets only used real rifles at the firing range. Guard duty was almost always carried out by first year students at the academy. Unless, like Porter, you had missed curfew or had accumulated excessive demerits. Then you were assigned Captain of the Guard, which meant you could amuse yourself by sending the plebes under your command on useless assignments.

The plebe ran up to Porter and snapped to attention.

Porter was in charge of two guards. He had already sent the first one to the academy library to make sure no one had stolen the massive painting of Oswald Cooper that hung high above the entrance.

"Hamilton," Porter said to the plebe. "I want you to double-time over to the west wall and make sure no cadet is trying to break curfew."

"Sir! Curfew is not for another five hours. Sir!"

"Excellent observation, Private Hamilton. But

some of our very fine seniors still get the little and big hands on their watches mixed up when telling time. Be on a special lookout for Cadet Reginald Reeves. Carry on."

"Yes, sir!" Hamilton double-timed back the way he had come.

Then Porter told Tommy what had happened last night.

Tommy listened slack-jawed to every last gory detail. When Porter had finished he said, "Get serious. Are you sure they *killed* him?"

"I swear on the ghost of Jeremiah Cooper, I saw it with my own two eyes. But what's weird is I haven't heard one damn word about it on the radio. Have you seen any newspapers today? I'm beginning to think that maybe the police didn't find the body."

"The police? I thought you weren't going to the police."

"Don't worry, big guy. I made a 911 call, but I remained anonymous."

"You think it might have been a goof?"

"What do you mean?"

"You know, a hustle to keep you from going to the police?"

"How would they know I was going to the police?"

"Maybe Booger told them," suggested Tommy.

"Hmmm . . . if it was an act, it was a damn good one." Porter still wasn't convinced. "I'm going to the Night Owl tonight after I get off guard duty. Back to the woods, you know, where it happened. Maybe the body's still there. Uh . . . can you come with me?"

Tommy shook his head. "Can't make it tonight, bud. Got a hot date."

"Damn," Porter muttered under his breath.

"But I can give you a ride up there after practice."

"Good enough."

"Besides, I can't wait to show you something I found at the Night Owl. Wait until you see it, it's so cool—you'll flip."

Porter's curiosity was peaked. "What is it?"

"You'll see," Tommy said with a sly grin as he jogged off in the direction of the gym.

Later that night, Porter followed Tommy up the stairs to the second floor of the Night Owl. The old wooden floor was scarred and creaky. Most of the crowd at the Night Owl hung out on the first floor where the pool tables and video games were. The second floor was more of a place for couples to sneak away to do a little necking in private. Porter could never remember being on the second floor. It seemed much larger than the first floor although that wasn't possible. They passed several doors until Tommy stopped in front of one in particular. "I found this the other night."

Porter looked at the locked door and then at Tommy. "Yeah? So? It's a locked door."

"Nope," Tommy corrected. "It just looks that way. Check this out." Tommy yanked down on the ancient padlock that locked the door. The lock snapped open. "This lock is so rusty, one yank and I broke it. No one can even tell it's broken unless you take a close look."

Porter gave Tommy a funny look. "So?"

Tommy gave Porter a little nudge in the ribs. "So, I thought this would be a great place to slip away with your little girlfriend for a little . . . you know."

Porter grinned. "Yeah . . . I know. Thanks, big guy. I'm sure I'll be spending a lot of time in that room. Ever hear of a motel?"

Tommy made a sour face. "Who has the money for that?"

"Yeah, I guess you're right. With all your gambling losses, you're lucky if you have enough money left to take a girl to a movie."

Tommy took a deep breath. Porter had struck a nerve. "You really know how to hurt a guy, bro."

"Sorry, big guy. I didn't mean anything by it—" Porter noticed a faint carving in the door. He blew some dust off it and took a closer look. It was a five-sided figure—a star inside a circle. He ran his finger over it. It suddenly felt hot to the touch. Porter quickly withdrew his finger.

"What's wrong?" Tommy asked.

"Nothing." Porter wasn't going to admit what had just happened to him. It was too weird to try to explain, especially to a dimwit like Tommy. But Tommy had also noticed the carving. "What is that thing?"

"I think it's a pentacle," Porter explained.

"A what?"

"It's a symbol witches use. Or used." Porter looked at Tommy who was now staring intently at the symbol. He seemed mesmerized by the pentacle. Porter had never seen his buddy concentrate this hard on anything that didn't have breasts.

"Used for what?" Tommy asked.

"Spells and stuff, I guess. I don't know. Whatever it is that witches do."

Tommy looked skeptical. He looked back at the pentacle. "C'mon. Probably some kid did it."

"I don't know," Porter said. "It looks pretty old."

Both Porter and Tommy were now staring at the pentacle.

"I'd stay out of this room if I were you," Porter said solemnly.

Seventeen

Porter used to enjoy hiking through the woods. He used to take the trail that linked the academy to the Night Owl Club on a regular basis before he got his car. It was about the only exercise he ever got.

But that was before he had witnessed a murder in those same woods. Now he knew the darkness hid evil. It hid violent forces, swift and terrible, that could take his life away. Porter felt alone and vulnerable. Every sound in the woods was magnified tenfold. He imagined things in the darkness that were on the prowl, watching him. He heard rustling behind every bush, in every tree branch. Twigs snapped at every turn. Instinct told him to turn around and run back to the light. To safety. To the Night Owl.

The Night Owl?

All of his troubles had begun in the Night Owl.

Maybe it was safer in the woods.

Except that it hadn't been safer for Booger.

Unless, like Tommy had said, it had all been a practical joke for his benefit. To scare him. And if it had been—it had certainly worked. Porter was definitely scared.

But Porter didn't think it was a joke. He stopped to get his bearings. It was stupid not to have brought a flashlight. Like so many other stupid things he had done lately. He found the trail he was looking for and walked to the spot where Booger had been murdered.

There was no corpse. Booger's body was missing.

He searched the area, and found no signs of the body. No signs of blood or brain matter or bits of shattered skull. At least none that he could see in the moonlight. They must've moved him. Or buried him somewhere.

Unless he had imagined it.

Porter hurried back to the Night Owl.

All of his troubles may have begun in the Night Owl, but he had also met Jamie there. The one bright light in this whole miserable affair. Maybe he had heard too many ghost stories about the Night Owl and was beginning to believe them. How else could he explain what had happened the other night? Skip had been sucked out that door. Not pushed out, not pulled out—*sucked out*. Now what the hell was that all about? Had he imagined it all?

He entered the Night Owl and headed for his booth.

And saw Red Jagger sitting at the bar.

Porter quickly disappeared into the crowded, smoke-filled Night Owl. He headed for the exit but stopped dead in his tracks when he saw Skip by the door, kicking and banging on a cigarette machine. Porter turned and ran the other way. He glanced over his shoulder and saw Red brusquely pushing his way through the crowd.

He was cornered.

He went up the stairs.

To the room with the pentacle.

The door was still unlocked, Porter noticed. Tommy must've forgotten to lock it again after showing it to him. Lucky for him. He stepped into the room and quietly pulled the door shut behind him. The old wooden planks of the floor seemed to groan in protest beneath his weight. Porter stared into the darkness. He felt as if he were staring into a vast black cavern, a cave.

An animal's den.

He heard a creaking sound.

And the animal was still in there. Lurking in the darkness.

The air had a sour, musky smell. A putrid smell. The smell of decay.

The moon, still fat and bright in the sky, shone through a grimy, soot-stained window. Porter stood perfectly still, barely breathing, and waited for his eyes to adjust to the darkness. He heard the creaking sound again. It was in the air. In front of him. Porter squinted in the darkness. He knew he should get the hell out of there, but he felt mesmerized, entranced.

There's something in this room.

As his eyes adjusted to the darkness, a form took shape in front of him. It was moving! Something was swinging back and forth. With a noose around its neck. Swinging from an overhead beam. The body slowly turned until it faced Porter, and he could clearly see the neat, almost perfectly round bullet hole in the middle of its forehead.

Porter was face to face with Booger.

Booger stared vacantly into the gloom with eyes opened wide in shock. In death. In horror. In outrage. His mouth opened as if to warn him.

Run.

Run!

Eighteen

Porter staggered backward. He felt the floor tilt at odd angles as if he were inside an amusement park funhouse. A House of Horrors. The body swung toward him, as if to grab him, and Porter jumped back. He turned away and ran to the door. As he reached for the door knob, he saw it move. Then the door began to open. Someone was coming in from the other side. He turned away from the door, his eyes quickly surveying the room. He saw another door. He ran to it and flung it open.

He heard a painful moan coming from inside the room.

He went in anyway. The door slammed shut behind him. *Must be the wind* Porter thought, trying to come up with a plausible explanation for it closing without him touching it.

He was engulfed in darkness. Then he felt a slight breeze. It grew into a blustery wind, and then, like a tornado, it lifted his body into the air and hurtled him through a series of open doors. This unseen force guided him through a labyrinth of back rooms until he was unceremoniously dumped at the head of a staircase. He scrambled to his feet and bolted down the stairs. It grew darker as he descended, and then he ran out of stairs.

This is too weird. Porter was panicked. He had to get out of this place before he went totally insane.

But how?

He was surrounded by darkness. The inky black darkness your eyes can never adjust to.

Porter felt something crawling on his back. His whole body became one gigantic goosebump. He felt a wrenching scream building in his gut. Just as he was about to lose control, he was pushed outside into the chilly night air.

He could see that he was outside the Night Owl. Pushed out by somebody or something? He had no idea. Porter sat on the wet grass, gulping in lungfuls of air, wondering what the hell had just happened to him. He turned around and looked at the grimy brick exterior of the Night Owl Club.

Pushed out of what?

There was no door.

Nineteen

Booger looked down at the deep scars of the old wooden floor in the Room of the Dead. It was stained deep with the ancient blood of its dreadful past. Spirits dwelled here, he somehow knew. Ghostly echoes of the past, who wouldn't mind a little company.

It was these spirits who had beckoned Booger.

Suddenly he heard flies, buzzing and fretting, as if around a moldering piece of dead meat. He listened as their complaints grew louder. Then he heard a noise, a creaking sound. They were coming, he knew. As sure as death. The world of the dead was opening; the crack growing wider. The air went sour. It turned thick and cold.

Almost here.

Booger choked back a gasp of horror.

They were here.

All around him. Mustn't show fear, must be strong, must not show revulsion, a tiny voice inside Booger's revived brain whispered to him. He closed his eyes and felt them gently running their tiny hands over his body. The tiny, charred hands of the children, the most hapless and innocent victims of the violent past; the children who had burned to their deaths when their orphanage had caught fire and swept them away in its fiery embrace. Some had died in that very room.

Enviously running their hands over his body, trying to remember what it was like to be alive, they whispered into his ear, their breath like flames. These innocent little waifs, who had for the past hundred years been damned to drift through the heavy fog of the undead, eternally yearned for the final darkness, the day when their restless souls could finally find sleep and peace.

Eloquent beyond words, the tiny voices spoke of wounds too painful to describe, of injustices that would never be avenged, of agonies no living mind could possibly hope to comprehend.

Booger listened, speechless, to their tales of torment.

He could do nothing else for their tortured souls except listen. And silently cry his grief. This was the price he must pay, he knew, for the chance to redeem himself. Or he would be doomed to join them. To walk with them forever.

Then the suffering hands and soft murmuring voices slowly fell away from him, reluctant to let go as if envious of those who were permitted to leave the Room of the Dead and return to the land of the living and light. The buzz of the fretting, complaining flies gradually subsided. The heavy, dank atmosphere of the room withdrew.

They were gone.

Booger slipped the noose off his neck and fell to the floor with a soft plop.

He couldn't hang around here all night.

He had things to do.

Twenty

Porter struggled to his feet. Out of habit, he limped in the direction of the parking lot before he remembered he didn't have his car anymore. It was a hunk of charred metal at the bottom of a ravine off Thirteen Bends Road. He turned and hurried toward the woods instead, ignoring the needles shooting through his ankle and foot and up his right leg. His head was hurting again, too. Had he banged it on something when he was pushed out of the Night Owl? Or was it from the knock on the head he got when the Jaggers ran him off the road? Or something else? Something he could never understand, even if he knew what it was—like the things that had been happening to him lately.

Porter looked back when he hit the edge of the woods. He saw no one following him.

He started to make his way, slowly and painfully, back to the academy as he tried to plan his next move. Should he go to the police? He had, after all, been a witness to a murder. He knew that for a fact, now, having just seen the corpse hanging upstairs in the Night Owl. But he had also just been pushed through a brick wall. How could he explain that to the police? Or to anyone? He couldn't even explain it to himself.

Going to the police would also mean having to look over his shoulder for the rest of his life, waiting for the day the Jaggers caught up to him—for the day when it would be his neck at the end of a noose.

The image of Booger swinging from the ceiling was so clear in his mind—even more clear now than when he'd seen it up close. It was as if the image had been stamped on the insides of his eyelids. Porter began to seriously think about getting out of town. Maybe Booger had had the right idea. If he wanted to live, he'd better make a run for it. He should've been on that Greyhound bus to New York a long time ago. He was lucky to have lived as long as he had. Why was he still hanging around Cooper Hollow, anyway? He didn't need the academy. And he didn't need college. He could make money anywhere. Money was the brutal bottom line. Money was what determined success or failure in the world. The world that he knew. And if you could make money in New York, you could make it anywhere . . .

His head started to pound.

The pain pulsated from the bump on his head. It was unbelievably fierce. Porter held his head as he dropped to his knees. The wind whipped up with frightening intensity. Porter fell on his back with his head still in his hands and watched the trees groan, the branches bending to the breaking point.

Then the night went black as the moon disappeared behind roiling clouds.

The wind, along with the pain in his head, slowly subsided. He got up off the ground and made his way back to the academy. He went into his room. Tommy was still out on his hot date. Porter pulled his duffel bag out of his locker and started stuffing things into it. He'd take just a few clothes, his computer disks, and a few other essentials. He could buy whatever else he needed in New York.

He would come back for Jamie later.

And there was something else he wanted to do— what was it? The throbbing in his head started up again. Worse than ever. It was hammering. Porter collapsed against his bed and rolled to the floor with his head held between his hands. He felt as if his skull was caving in upon itself. Crushing the life out of him. He lay on the floor writhing in pain until the throbbing passed.

He remembered what else it was he had wanted to do. He had to call the police. Booger's body was still hanging in a back room at the Night Owl. He couldn't leave it there. Who knows if anyone would ever find it. He supposed the smell would eventually give it away. Still, the kid deserved a decent burial.

He sat on the edge of the bed and waited for his head to clear. Then he went down the hallway to the public phones at the end of the wing and punched in 911.

"Nine-one-one. Sergeant Futrynzski."

"Yes, ah . . . there's a body in the Night Owl."

There was a long pause. "Is this the kid from last night?"

"I beg your pardon?"

"The kid who called about a body in the woods?"

151

"Yes, sir."

"Listen, kid. Don't be tying up the line with this kind of nonsense—"

"It's not nonsense, sir," Porter insisted. "There's been a murder. And the body was moved to a back room on the second floor of the Night Owl. It's the same body."

"You know we could arrest you for this—false alarms are against the law—"

"For real—there's a body there! Take the back staircase, its four or five doors down, on the right side. There's a pentacle carved into the door."

"A what?"

"A pentacle. A star inside a circle. It means . . . well, never mind what it means—could you just check it out, sir? Please?"

"All right," came the skeptical reply. "We'll check it out. Can you tell us who the victim is?"

"It's . . . Booger."

"Who?"

"I mean . . . Burger. Freddy Burger I think his name is. He was murdered by the Jaggers."

"Skip and Red Jagger?"

"Yes, sir. Do you know them?"

"For years, unfortunately. And what's your name, kid?"

"How do you know I'm a kid?"

"You sound like a kid."

Porter made a mental note to learn how to disguise his voice on the phone. Porter had no intention of giving the cops his name. He was about to make up an alias when the throbbing pain in his head started up again.

"What did you say your name was again," came the sergeant's voice as if from the opposite end of a long tunnel.

"Smith," Porter blurted out. It was as if he had lost control of his voice. The words tumbled out without passing through his brain. "I go to the Hudson Military Academy—" He abruptly hung up.

What the hell was he doing? He hadn't meant to give the police any information about himself.

The pain in his head was spreading across the back of his head and down his neck.

Porter went back to his room and sat on the edge of his bed. The bump on his head seemed to be getting larger. He felt light-headed, faint. Maybe he'd better take it easy for a few days. Just hang out at the academy and rest up.

He could always catch the bus to New York later.

Tuesday morning

Porter woke up to a banging on his door. Tommy was snoring loudly in his bunk by the window. Porter got up and slipped on his flip-flops. He shuffled over to the door and opened it. Sergeant Saunders loomed in front of him, the ever present cigar clenched between his large, square teeth. Behind him stood a very officious looking older man in a baggy gray suit. He was a big man with a beer gut, and Porter had to look up to see his face—something he rarely had to do since he was so tall himself.

"You've got company, dumbhead!" Saunders shouted, despite the early hour. He obviously didn't

153

care if he woke up the entire dormitory. "This is Detective Bronson of the Cooper Hollow Police Department. He wants to have a little chat with you. In my office—NOW!"

"Yes, sir," Porter said, and the two men left. He closed the door and dressed quickly.

Bleary-eyed, Tommy rolled over in his bunk and looked at Porter. "Who the hell was that?"

"A cop."

"Huh?" Tommy asked, sitting up on the edge of the bed suddenly wide awake.

"I said, a cop," Porter said nonchalantly.

"What the hell does he want?" Tommy asked anxiously.

"I don't know," Porter said with a shrug.

"Just play it cool, little buddy," Tommy warned.

Porter finished dressing and double-timed down to Saunders' office. He knocked on the door and Saunders' gruff voice ordered him in. Porter entered the office and snapped to attention in front of the sergeant's desk. Saunders took his time pouring a cup of coffee for the detective while Porter stood rigidly at attention. He handed Bronson the cup before sitting down in his swivel chair behind the desk. The detective was sitting on the edge of the desk regarding Porter with a critical eye.

Porter watched Bronson out of the corner of his eye as the big cop gave him the once over. He seemed too old to be a detective. His hair was nearly entirely gray, almost white, and Porter guessed that the suit he had on was out of style even before Porter was born. Porter could tell by the way he was glaring at him that the detective assumed all boys his age were either high on drugs or just naturally wacko.

Bronson glanced at a little notepad that he held in his hand. "Did you make a 911 call at 9:36 P.M. last night?"

Porter hesitated. A nerve in his forehead twitched. "No, sir."

Bronson looked back at his notes. "No?"

"No, sir," Porter repeated.

"We had a report of a murder," the big cop went on, looking at his notepad. "The caller identified himself as Smith and the victim as a kid named Fred Burger. You didn't make that call?"

"No, sir."

A slender slice of pain, intense but delicate, began to grow inside his head.

Saunders leaned back in his swivel chair and sucked on his cigar as if he hadn't a care in the world. But Porter knew he was taking everything in. After their first conversation, Porter realized that the sarge wasn't the dumb ex-leatherneck most of the cadets thought he was.

"Any idea who could've made that phone call?" Bronson asked.

"No, sir. Probably one of the guys here at the academy playing a prank—"

"This was no prank, son," the big cop said curtly, standing up.

"I'm sorry I can't help you. I don't know anything about a murder, sir."

Saunders stopped puffing on his cigar. He sat up straight in his swivel chair and focused his attention on Porter. "What's going on, Smith?"

"Beg your pardon, sir?"

"Are you involved in something you shouldn't be?"

Porter said nothing.

"Did you or did you not make that phone call?" Saunders pressed on.

"No, sir." Porter felt the pain inside his head start to throb.

"Why would someone use your name?" Bronson asked.

"I don't know, sir. I'm . . . I'm not the most popular guy on campus."

"And why is that?" the cop asked.

"I guess I'm not an institution man, sir. The other cadets resent that. They don't think I belong here."

Bronson looked over at Saunders.

"I can vouch for him on that one," Saunders said. "He's a bit slack in the leadership department. His grades are topnotch, and his school records show he has a very high I.Q." Saunders took a puff on his cigar. "Although he hasn't displayed much of it around here lately."

"What do you mean, Sergeant?" the detective asked.

"The guard caught him trying to sneak back over the wall Saturday night. He was late returning to the base and was out past curfew."

Bronson turned his attention back to Porter. "Why were you out so late, young man?"

"I had a car accident, sir. Totalled my vehicle."

"Where?"

"On Thirteen Bends Road?"

"That's pretty close to the Night Owl, isn't it?"

"Yes, sir, it runs right past it."

The detective wrote something down. "Did you report the accident?"

"No."

"Why not?"

"I don't know." Porter decided not to use the 'I-was-in-shock' excuse with the detective.

"Oh, c'mon, son. You can do better than that," the detective said. "Did someone try to run you off the road? Is that what happened?"

Porter felt clammy all over. He wished he could sit down. He didn't want the detective and Sergeant Saunders to see him trembling. "No, sir." The throbbing in his head grew more intense.

Bronson stood up and breathed out heavily. He came into Porter's field of vision. He was standing very close to him now. "Do you know Skip and Red Jagger?" he asked. Porter could smell the coffee on his breath.

Porter felt his forehead bead up with sweat. "Not personally. I've, uh . . . heard of them."

"Just *heard* of them?" Bronson snapped. He looked at his little notepad. "They weren't sitting with you in a booth at this club last Friday night?"

Porter clenched his teeth. The detective had caught him in a lie. So Bronson had checked up on him. Porter realized he could have been seen in the Night Owl with the Jaggers by any number of people.

"Uh . . . Friday, did you say?"

"Yes, Friday."

"Friday's are usually pretty crowded. I may have shared my table with them."

Bronson referred to his notepad. "Did you and

157

Skip Jagger get into an argument over something last Friday night? While sitting at the booth?"

"No sir, not that I can remember."

"You can't remember?"

"No, sir."

"You didn't get into an argument with Skip Jagger and leave the club?"

"I may have left the club, sir, but I don't remember getting into an argument—"

"And then maybe the Jaggers were waiting for you outside the club or on Thirteen Bends Road somewhere between the Night Owl Club and the academy—he knew you would be coming back that way—and things got a little rough. Rough enough to run you off the road. Is that what happened, Smith?"

"No, sir."

Bronson was now standing very close to Porter, almost nose to nose. "So you decided to get revenge on the Jaggers. Is that what happened, Mr. Smith?"

It took a moment to sink in. "Did you say revenge, sir?"

"That's correct, cadet."

Revenge? "I don't understand," Porter began, puzzled. "You mean something happened to Skip and Red Jagger?"

"If you call getting your head twisted around backward *something.* They were found upstairs at the Night Owl. They're dead, and I think you know all about it."

"I d-didn't—" Porter stammered.

"Now let me get this straight," the detective said.

"You didn't make that 911 call, and you didn't know the Jaggers were murdered until just now?"

"Yes, sir. I mean . . . c'mon, look at me. I probably couldn't land a punch on either of the Jaggers, much less kill them. Do I look like a head-twisting kind of guy to you? And if I did, why would I call 911 and report it?"

The detective leaned back on Saunders' desk, took a sip of his coffee. "If you're as smart as Sergeant Saunders claims you are, you might have hired someone else to do it for you. Then maybe you called 911 and gave your own name to divert suspicion from yourself."

"Then why would I deny calling it in now?"

"Maybe you thought about it and realized it wasn't such a good idea after all, so now you're backpeddling. Or maybe you panicked when you made the call and are trying to cover up now. Is that the way it is, son?"

"No, sir."

The pain in Porter's head started to hammer away so intensely, he flinched from the pain. He felt as if the floor were slipping out from under his feet. He started to sway a little. Saunders came around his desk quickly and caught Porter before he fell. "Are you all right, Smith?" he asked, pulling over a chair for him to sit in.

Porter sat down and rubbed his head, which felt as if it were about to explode. "I'm just feeling a little woozy, sir. You know, from my car accident." His head hurt like hell and the room was starting to swim around in a foggy haze. He could almost feel the knot on his head *growing*.

Saunders looked at Bronson. "Maybe we should finish this interview at a later time, Detective."

The detective reluctantly stepped away from the desk. "No problem, Sergeant," Bronson said, nodding politely. "That'll give me time to do a little more checking up on this young man's story."

He removed a large, slightly frayed trench coat from the coat rack in the corner, and looked over at Porter as he buttoned it up. "My guess is that whoever killed those boys did us all a big favor. But murder's still a crime, and it's my job to find out who did it. And until I do, young man, you're not to leave Cooper Hollow. Understood?"

"Yes, sir," Porter rasped. His head felt as if it were cracking open like a raw egg.

After the detective had left, Saunders returned to his swivel chair. "You want to talk about any of this, dumbhead?"

"No, sir," Porter said, gritting his teeth from the pain in his head. "I . . . I can't. Right now."

There was a moment of silence. "Don't wait until your ass is too deep into something before you decide to crawl out, Smith," Saunders warned. "It may be too late by then."

"Yes, sir."

Later that evening Porter was back on the trail through the woods to the Night Owl. He was surprised that Saunders hadn't laid some extra guard duty on him just to loosen up his tongue a little. But apparently the sarge was going to let him work his problem out his own way. If Porter had asked Saunders why, he probably would have received a long lecture on the merits of leadership and the obligations of a young man to accept responsibility and commitment to duty—blah, blah, blah. And he didn't have time for lectures.

He hoped Jamie was waiting for him at the Night Owl. He missed her. Ironically, this time he had stood her up. At least he had a good excuse. Except she would never believe what had happened to him at the Night Owl last night. Who would?

Booger and the Jaggers—all murdered.

There was definitely something weird going on in that club.

And not just the murders. Something . . . unearthly. He tried to make sense of the last few nights. He had tried to convince himself during a sleepless night that he was just stressed out. Or that the injury to his head was more serious than he had thought.

He *tried* to convince himself of that.

Unless the Night Owl really was haunted—the Nightmare Club. Behind every locked door at the club was a nightmare waiting to happen.

And he had walked into his.

At least there was no longer any reason to run. The guys chasing him were dead. And he wouldn't confide in the police, either. He had already gotten a little taste of the police from Detective Bronson, and it left a sour taste in his mouth. If Bronson exposed his involvement with the Jaggers, he would be kicked out of the academy for sure. And he could kiss Harvard goodbye.

Yeah, the less he had to do with the police, the better.

A throbbing bolt of pain shot through his head with the suddenness of a thunderclap. He pressed the sides of his head with the palms of his hands. He wanted to pop the pain right out through his ears.

The migraine passed.

Damn concussion.

Porter arrived at Night Owl and made his way through the club to his booth, keeping a wary eye open for Jamie. Maybe she'd be waiting for him at his booth. Porter looked across the crowded room, his eyes searching for Jamie.

There *was* someone waiting for him, but it wasn't Jamie.

Porter recognized the Red Devils baseball cap and matching school jacket.

But it can't be, Porter thought in amazement.

He's dead.

Twenty-one

At first Porter thought he was hallucinating. Just when he was becoming used to the throbbing migraines, he wondered if now he'd have to adjust to seeing things. Like a ghost, for instance.

Porter took a closer look. There was no doubt in Porter's mind that it was Booger. The red and white Red Devils cap was pulled down low so the visor brushed his eyebrows. The jacket collar was pulled up.

Booger looked up as Porter approached the booth. His complexion was pale, but his voice was clear and strong. "What's happening, dude?" Booger gave Porter a friendly smile. "Hey, that lump on your forehead is the size of a tomato. You'd better sit down before you fall down."

Porter sat down, lightly touching the discolored knob on his forehead as he did so. "Yeah, I had a little accident," he said, looking at Booger closely. "And you?"

Booger only grinned.

Porter continued to stare at Booger, trying to decide if he was sitting with a ghost. How could you determine something like that? He wondered if he would be able to see Booger's reflection in a mirror.

"You probably thought I was dead, right?" Booger asked, as if reading his mind.

"Well . . . yeah."

There was an awkward silence as Porter tried to get a closer look at Booger, whose face drifted in and out of shadows created by the flickering candle light. "You got scammed back there in the woods, Porter. There were blanks in the gun and the hanging was rigged. The Jaggers faked my murder and forced me to go along with it. They wanted to scare you to keep you from going to the police. You were making too much money for them to just let you go."

Porter was skeptical. "When they ran me off Thirteen Bends Roads, was that a con too?"

Booger only shrugged. "I couldn't tell you about that. Maybe they just got a little carried away, who knows? Maybe your driving sucks. But that doesn't matter now. They're dead, and you're alive. And I'm here to try to keep it that way."

"Keep *me* alive?" Porter asked, confused. "What about yourself?"

"Don't worry about me. Remember back at the Greyhound Station, when you gave me all your money?"

Porter nodded.

"Well, I owe you one."

"Says who?"

"Some friends of mine."

Porter didn't think of Booger as the type of guy

who had friends. "Thanks, but—no offense—I don't see how you can help."

"Listen, this is serious. Your life's in danger."

"From who?" Porter asked, humoring Booger.

"Whoever killed the Jaggers will kill you, too."

Porter sat in stunned silence for a moment. "Says who?"

"Friends of mine."

"Who are these *friends?*" This cloak of mystery was annoying Porter.

"I don't think you'd want to meet them."

If they're anything like the Jaggers, he's probably right, Porter thought. Still, he was beginning to suspect that Booger was just a disturbed young man out for some attention. He wasn't making a hell of a lot of sense, that was for sure. Porter wondered if Booger was on crystal meth, like Skip Jagger, or some other drug. He tried to see if Booger's pupils were dilated, but all he saw was his own reflection staring back at him. "What's going on, Booger?"

"I have to pay back my debt to you before I go."

"You don't owe me anything."

"It's them I owe."

"Who—oh yeah, I know, those *friends* of yours." There was another moment of icy silence. "And you won't tell me who these friends are?"

"I told you, you wouldn't want to know. But they told me your life is in danger. And believe me, they oughta know."

Porter looked at Booger suspiciously. Could he trust him?

"You have one chance to live, Porter. And the odds

are against you. But we have to find out who the murderer is before he kills you."

This kid wasn't all too bright to begin with. Now he's totally over the edge, Porter thought. Maybe that fake hanging cut his air off for too long, some brain cells got damaged. Still, no harm in humoring him. "So, ah . . . did these friends of yours give you any clue as to who this guy might be?"

"No. I think they're leaving that up to us to find out. But I do have one lead."

"Let's hear it, Sherlock."

"Friday night I saw someone in here I thought I recognized. I had seen him once before when I was with the Jaggers in New York City. I only caught a glimpse of him, but you can't miss him, he's such a big guy."

"Do you know his name?"

"His name is Meat Bomb Barker."

Porter tried to keep his fear from showing. He remembered what Tommy had told him about the biker. "And you think this guy killed the Jaggers?"

"He had a good reason. They murdered his little brother."

Something inside of Porter simply refused to believe all this craziness was happening to him. "Are you sure about that?" Porter hadn't totally believed Tommy's story. Maybe Booger heard it from the same unreliable source.

"I'm sure."

"Or is this something else your *friends* told you about?"

"No, I saw this."

Porter looked at Booger in disbelief. "You were a witness to murder?"

"No, I wasn't a witness. I was an *accomplice.*"

"What?"

"Did that lump on your head affect your hearing? I said I helped them do it."

Porter felt his skin crawl. "Get out of here," he said, shaking his head. "I don't believe this."

"I held the guy down as they strangled him. I handed them the knife they used to hack the guy to pieces. I held the Hefty Bags open while they stuffed his body parts inside. I helped them drag the bags down to their car. I helped them load the bags into the trunk. I drove down to the Hudson River with them and helped them dump the body."

Porter stared back at Booger, horrified.

"I told you they had something on me," Booger said.

Porter felt dizzy.

"If that guy was Meat Bomb, and I think it was, he saw us all sitting together in this booth. He's going to assume you're part of the Jagger gang."

"You mean . . ."

"I mean he's going to kill you," Booger said. "If he can."

Porter fought back the panic surging through him. "It can't be the same guy. He's in jail, isn't he?"

"He could've made bail. Or his lawyer could have gotten him out somehow. Who knows? It happens every day. But the point is—he's here *now.* And we have to do something about it."

Porter was taken aback. The false sense of security Porter had felt after learning of the Jaggers' death had disappeared. He looked into Booger's eyes which had taken on a strange, depthless quality. There was a glint about them, like a cat's eyes when a light shone on them.

"And if Meat Bomb isn't the murderer?"

"Then I don't know who else it could be.

Porter saw Jamie enter the room.

She was so drop-dead pretty it rattled his mind just to look at her. She stopped just inside the doorway and glanced around the room. Looking for him, he hoped. He abruptly stood up, nearly toppling the booth table, and waved to her.

But she didn't see him.

She started talking to someone sitting in the corner booth. Porter scrambled out from behind the booth table, completely forgetting about Booger, and made his way across the floor. Seeing Jamie had forced all thoughts of murder and danger from his mind.

A herd of jocks from Cooper Hollow High suddenly entered the room laughing loudly and made their way to the snack bar, blocking Porter. He pushed through them, anxious to see Jamie. He hadn't realized how much he missed her until this moment. Missed her so much it hurt. He wanted to gather her up in his arms and squeeze her. He wanted to kiss her and to hold her and feel her warmth and her heartbeat and to taste her tongue. He hurried across the crowded room with anticipation welling up inside of him.

But Jamie had disappeared.

Twenty-two

"What's up, little buddy?" came a voice from the corner booth.

Porter looked over and saw Tommy sitting by himself in the booth with that glassy look in his eyes he got after knocking back a few. Porter suspected Tommy had been drinking heavily before coming to the Night Owl. He was probably worried about getting expelled from his precious academy.

"Have a seat, bud. Let's celebrate," Tommy said.

"Celebrate what?"

"Didn't you hear?" Tommy asked. "Someone knocked off the Jaggers."

Tommy had already gone to his first class by the time Porter returned to their room after his grilling by Detective Bronson. Porter didn't have a chance to tell him that he himself was the number one suspect.

"Isn't that great news, Porter?" Tommy asked.

"It sure is, big guy," Porter said. "But I can't celebrate it right now. I've got to find Jamie."

Tommy chuckled. "You mean Ms. Beeswax?"

"That's right, big guy. My hot little honey."

"Sorry, bud. I just saw her leave with another guy."

Porter's face drained of color.

Tommy laughed. "Just kidding little buddy. She just asked me if I had seen you. I thought you were pulling extra guard duty so I made a little joke and told her I thought you were upstairs in the room with . . . the whatchamacallit . . . the pentacle—where those two creeps got what was coming to them."

"You told her I was in the Pentacle Room?"

"Yup." Tommy made a pumping motion with his hand. "I told her you were up there playing with yourself." He laughed loudly.

Porter turned to leave.

"Hey, little buddy?" Tommy's voice brought Porter back.

"You taking any action now?"

"Can't do it right now, big guy," Porter said, anxious to leave. He wanted to stop Jamie before she reached the Pentacle Room.

"Oh," Tommy said with disappointment. Then he gave Porter an exaggerated wink. He was really loaded. "Because I wanted to make a little bet that you might need *this* tonight." He reached into his shirt pocket and pulled out a condom. He wiggled it in front of Porter with a lopsided grin. "But you know what a loser I am."

Porter grinned. "Ah . . . thanks anyway, big guy. Got my own," he said, returning the wink with a giant one of his own. Then he headed for the nearest staircase, taking the steps two and three at a time until he reached the upper floor. He came to an

170

abrupt stop, feeling suddenly lost. Maybe it was the bad light, or he needed new glasses, or the fact that he was seldom on the upper floor, but he felt as if he had suddenly stepped into another dimension. The old wooden floor was washed with a pale, yellow moonlight that fought its way through the dirty, grimy windows. He seemed to be in the middle of a wheel, the spokes were the corridors that led away from the hub. The wheel was turning.

Slowly revolving before his eyes.

Porter closed his eyes and shook his head. He opened his eyes, and the room had stopped moving. In fact, it was a different room altogether. Should have taken the back stairs instead of this one, Porter realized, a little too late, as he squeezed his eyes shut and opened them again. Now the room was many rooms, a big and sprawling set of squares that seemed to multiply like mirror images of itself. One room led into another which led to another which led to another, making Porter's head spin. The room slowly returned to normal.

Porter looked around.

He saw a couple necking in a dark corner, deep in the shadows. They made him think of the last time he had seen Jamie—when they had kissed. Had she made out with him only because she was lonely? he wondered. A new girl in a new town, a little wild, desperate for a little company? Porter knew better than most what it was like to be so lonely you craved company—and anybody would do. He had never really had a girlfriend. He had almost given up. Till he met Jamie. She had changed the way he thought about everything.

And he had thought it was only money that could do that.

Had Jamie come to the Night Owl to tell him it was over? Probably, Porter thought, feeling sorry for himself. She must have met a guy at school she really liked—some big jock. The hurt burned deep inside of him, and he knew it wouldn't go away for a long, long time. Well, at least Tommy hadn't gotten her, he consoled himself, as his eyes scanned the room trying to spot her. He was distracted by a rattling sound.

What the hell was that?

It sounded like a chain. Then he heard laughter, or something that sounded like laughter, followed by a loud, harsh bark. But it didn't sound like any dog he had ever heard. He felt a chill of fear. He turned around and headed back down the stairs.

He didn't get very far.

Blocking his way was a big, wide, hairy, ugly, mean-looking man. He wore a pair of greasy bib overalls, with no shirt underneath. A sleeveless leather vest barely covered the upper half of his body. Clumps of black frizzy chest hair jutted above his overalls in such abundance it was hard to tell where the hair left off and the black leather vest began. His beard looked like steel wool and obscured most of his face and neck. But what frightened Porter the most was the large tattoo he saw on the man's big, fat, quivering bicep. It was crude and homemade, the kind of tattoo cons in prison made for each other. A tattoo of an exploding piece of meat.

Porter was face to face with Meat Bomb Barker.

His large barrel chest took up almost the entire

width of the stair. Porter knew that getting past this guy on the stairs would prove to be almost impossible, even if he let him by. Porter watched his two big hands tug at the bannister, as if he needed the extra leverage to pull his large frame up the stairs. The fingers were big and meaty, the size of breakfast sausages, and he could easily imagine them wrapped around his neck.

Porter hurried back up the stairs.

Porter looked around and everything seemed different from just a few moments before. The second floor was now a pentagon. How could this be? He heard a creaking sound on the stairs behind him. There was one long, dark corridor. Porter stared into the darkness as the creaking on the stairs grew louder, came closer. His heart was pounding, as if to keep pace with the throbbing in his head. He felt strange and disjointed in the gloomy darkness that spread out before him. Suddenly the little square patch of light that was the top of the stairs went black.

Porter bolted down the corridor. There was no other way to go. He entered the first room that he came to, opened and closed the door as quietly as he could and leaned against it. He held his breath as lumbering footsteps came his way. Then he heard something else. From *inside* the room. It sounded like children whispering secrets. He looked over his shoulder and stared into the darkness but could see nothing.

Then he heard a noise outside the door.

A wheezing sound. A man's labored breathing. Porter cocked his head back in the direction of the noise and listened. He could smell the sour odor of Meat Bomb's sweat right through the thick wooden door.

He felt something rubbing on his neck.

Gently. Almost tickling him. Then breath as cold as ice that smelled of mustard whispered into his ear. Porter gasped with horror and stood frozen to the floorboards. His heart was slamming so hard against his ribs he feared it might punch a hole in his chest. The unseen terror spoke to him. "Don't run."

Then he heard a soft thumping, squishing sound as whatever it was drifted away from him.

Porter glanced over his shoulder and saw two luminous red eyes looking back at him with the ravenous gaze of a hungry animal. He wrenched open the door with such fury it banged the wall like a rifle shot. He shot out of the room and made a hysterical flight back down the corridor. He'd take his chances with Meat Bomb. Or the police. Or God Himself. Anything was better than staying in that room with that thing. He bolted back down the stairs and into the noisy first floor interior. He stopped and looked fearfully back up the stairs, his hands still grasping the wooden stair bannister with sweaty palms. He waited for his senses, still sluggish with shock, to function normally again.

He felt a hand placed upon his shoulder.

The breath hissed out of him, and his body went rigid as a voice whispered his name.

Twenty-three

It was Jamie.

Porter was so glad to see her. And she looked so beautiful in her tight jeans and loose silky, black blouse. Porter wanted to touch the soft material and feel her skin beneath it, but he was afraid she didn't want him to, so he did nothing.

Jamie looked at Porter expectantly. "Don't just stand there you jerk. Kiss me," she said.

Porter scooped her up in his arms and kissed her. She smelled fresh and clean. Soapy. Her shaggy brown hair had a bright sheen to it and smelled faintly of lemons. This must be what heaven is like, Porter thought. It took all of his willpower not to run his hands up and under that blouse to her bare skin. Finally, they broke for air.

"I take it you missed me," Jamie said.

"Oh, man, did I ever."

"Where have you been?" she asked. "I was looking all over for you last night. Tonight, too."

"In hell," Porter said, his adrenaline still pumping. He looked fearfully over his shoulder, up the stairs.

"Why, what's the matter?" Jamie asked, growing worried.

"Someone is after me."

"Someone . . ." Jamie looked up the stairs. "Who? The Invisible Man?" She gave Porter a funny look. "You haven't been drinking have you?"

"No way," Porter said. "C'mon, I want you to meet someone." He took her by the hand and led her back to the booth. He knew that Jamie didn't believe half of what he had told her about his gambling operation and his involvement with the Jaggers. Not that he could blame her. He didn't exactly look like your typical gambling czar. But maybe she would believe Booger.

But Booger was gone.

Porter looked about.

"Still looking for the invisible man?" Jamie said with an impish grin.

"No, Booger."

"Who?"

"You know, that guy I told you about. The kid with the Jaggers. He was killed, then he came alive again. Only he says it never happened—"

"Porter," Jamie said with a concerned look. "I think you'd better sit down." They slid into the booth seat but Porter was too nervous to sit still. He kept looking around the room—he half expected the gates of hell to open in front of him, unleashing its horde of demons upon him.

Jamie's cool touch on his forehead brought him back to reality. "You feel a little feverish. Are you sure you're all right? What's this lump?" she asked, concerned.

"It's . . . nothing."

"What happened to you anyway?" Jamie asked, running her fingertips gently over the scratches on Porter's face.

"Remember I told you about the Jaggers?"

"Yeah."

"Did you hear about those two guys that got murdered here last night?"

"Three guys," Jamie said.

"No, it was only two."

"I heard three. Everyone's talking about it around here."

"Did you know the victims were the Jaggers?"

"You mean the ones that were blackmailing you?"

"Yeah."

"They were killed in that room up there?"

"Yes."

"I was just up there—I didn't go in. I just went up there to look around. All I saw was a door covered with a lot of yellow tape. Some guy told me you went up there."

"That's my roommate, Tommy Wilson. Stay away from him."

"Why?"

"He's a pervert."

Jamie raised her eyebrows. "So how does he know me?"

"I told him about you when I got the warning in the showers."

"What warning?"

"That you were in danger."

"Me?" Jamie asked, more annoyed than frightened. "Why am I in danger?"

177

"The Jaggers were using you to get to me. They said if I didn't do what they said, they would mess you up."

Jamie gave Porter a long look. "Was this before or after you told me you were going to the police?"

"After."

"Did you ever go to the police like you said you would?"

Porter hesitated. "I talked to them." His head started to throb.

Jamie looked skeptical. "When?"

Porter felt a stab of pain in the lump in his head as if someone had just driven a spear through his skull. He squeezed his eyes shut from the pain.

"When?" Porter heard Jamie's voice as if it were coming from a great distance.

"This morning."

"This morning . . . you said you were going last Friday night. Right after I left you."

"I—I couldn't, Jamie. Things got out of hand—"

Jamie looked down in disappointment. "Porter . . . you lied to me. The first promise you ever made to me, and you broke it. How could you?"

"Jamie, listen, I—I didn't go because I was afraid of what they might do to you—"

"Oh c'mon Porter," Jamie shot back. "Don't use me as an excuse. You didn't go because you were scared. Scared of losing your precious gambling operation. Scared you might not make enough money off your classmates to put yourself through some fancy Ivy League school." Jamie's outburst stung Porter because it was so close to the truth. But now it wasn't the money he was afraid of losing. It was Jamie.

"I'm not scared . . ." He had to think about that one. "Well, I am, but not the way you think."

"You're just a scared, rotten liar." Jamie was on the verge of tears.

"I am not a liar . . ." The damn throbbing. "I would have gone to the police, but I was afraid for you." The throbbing got worse.

"Really?" Jamie asked. "It wasn't because you were afraid of getting kicked out of your stupid academy? Or because of some ridiculous promise you made to your father? Did you even make that promise to your father on his deathbed? Or was that another lie?"

"That was the truth," Porter assured her.

"But the Jaggers are dead now, right?"

"I hope so," Porter said in a quiet voice.

"So there's no reason why you can't go to the police now, is there?"

"There's a very good reason."

"What?"

"They think *I* killed them!"

"Did you?"

"That hurt."

"Did you or didn't you?"

"No. Of course not. Do you think I did?"

"I don't know. I can't tell when you're telling the truth anymore."

"I'm telling the truth . . ." Porter saw Booger. "This guy will back me up." Porter stood and waved for Booger to come over. He would set her straight. But Booger only smiled back at him.

179

"Who are you waving to?" she asked.

"Booger."

"What does he look like?" Jamie asked following Porter's line of sight.

"He's wearing a Red Devils cap and jacket. Can't you see him?"

"No."

"He's right over there!" Porter said, exasperated. "Hey Booger!" Some people looked over. "Booger!"

"Porter, sit down. People are staring."

"Hey Booger . . ." Porter continued to wave madly trying to get Booger to come over to the booth. But Booger had disappeared. "Maybe I should go after him."

"Please, Porter," Jamie said as she tugged on his sleeve, trying to get him to sit down. By now everyone in the club was staring at them. Porter reluctantly sat down. Jamie was silent for a moment, then she said, "You know, when I first saw you, I thought you were different from most of the guys I had dated. You stuck up for me at the pool table, you were funny, sincere—you even seemed smart. But you're not so different, after all. You're just a jerk like all the others. A jerk and a liar . . ." Jamie got up to leave. Tears glistened in her eyes.

Porter stood up. "Jamie, wait! I'm not a liar . . ." The room started to tilt at weird angles and the throbbing in his head got worse. He sat back down and waited for his head to clear. Then he went after Jamie. He looked for her everywhere, but he couldn't find her. He was standing in the middle of the billiards room feeling like a lost child when he heard a voice call his name. He looked over and saw Reggie Reeves standing by a pool table, chalking up his stick.

"Lose your way, Smith?"

Porter walked over to him. "I was looking for Jamie. Did you see her?"

"You mean that little cheating piece of ass that owes me money?"

Porter tried to control his anger. "Yeah. Did you see her?"

"What's it matter to a fag like you? Everyone at the academy knows you're a homo. You and your white trash lover boy, Tommy Wilson—"

Enough was enough. Porter hammered an overhand right to the point of Reggie's chin, putting plenty of weight behind it, the way Tommy had shown him. The punch landed solidly. Reggie staggered backward, bounced off the pool table, where Porter nailed him a second time with a vicious left hook. Reggie fell to the floor with a thud, his pool stick clattering after him.

Porter shook his right hand, which hurt like hell. But it was worth it.

He quickly left the billiards room to the murmuring of the crowd and went to the bar. He found Jenny Demos. "Jenny . . ."

"Oh, hi, Porter," she said with a bright smile.

"Hi, Jenny."

"You're getting to be a stranger sitting over there in your booth every night."

Porter used to chat fairly frequently with Jenny when things were slow. That was before he took over the corner booth to conduct his business a little more discreetly. Then Porter had a sudden and strange revelation. Since he had started running his gambling operation out of the corner booth, he had never seen anyone else sitting there. Even on crowded nights, his booth was always empty, as if waiting for him to arrive.

"Jenny? I, ah . . ." He didn't know where to start. "Do you know a kid named Booger?"

"You mean Freddy Burger?"

"Yeah."

Jenny's eyes glowed with a strange light. "I see him around every now and then."

"Did you see him earlier tonight?"

"No." She fixed Porter with a mysterious smile. "But you might check upstairs."

He'd pass on that. "Did you see a really big guy? He looked like a biker. He has a tattoo right here," Porter said, pointing to his bicep.

"He was in earlier." Jenny filled an empty basket with some tortilla chips and put out some salsa.

"Do you . . . know the guy?" Porter asked.

"He was hanging around here the past few nights, but I can't say that I know him. Nor would I want to. Some people give off bad vibes, know what I mean?"

"Yeah." Did he ever.

"But he left this," Jenny said, sliding over a match-book. "Excuse me, Porter."

Porter wanted to talk to Jenny some more, but the bar had gotten busy. He wanted to ask her why his life had suddenly become such a mind-boggling mess. Had this stuff really happened or was it just some crazy hallucination he was having?

He looked at the matchbook. *The Savage Limbo.*

It was a bar on the Lower East Side of Manhattan.

Porter stuffed the matchbook into his jacket pocket as he walked outside. He watched the wind whip back the branches of the crooked, leafless, dead-looking trees that grew around the Night Owl Club.

The Savage Limbo.

It was what his life had become.

Twenty-four

It was late. Very late. But Porter didn't feel like sleeping. He paced his room in the dark, fumbling with the book of matches that Jenny had given him. He'd better come up with a plan soon, before his world crumpled down around him like a flimsy sand castle.

That thing on the second floor of the Night Owl. What the hell was that?

Part of the brain damage he must be suffering? Who could make sense of this? He was beginning to believe all the horror stories about the Night Owl Club might be true. The Nightmare Club. He had seen some of those nightmares. They had even spoken to him.

Don't run.

They'd be punching his ticket to the funny farm if he didn't get his thinking straightened out. Maybe, hopefully, it was just that lump on his head. He had a concussion, and he was stressed out, and he was imagining things. So why did that lump on his head keep growing? Like Pinocchio's nose.

Maybe he really was going insane.

Maybe he was already there.

He continued to pace, afraid to leave the room. The world outside had become a shooting gallery to him. He felt like a duck at a carnival sideshow. He wondered who would get the teddy bear for blowing his brains out. Looking out his window, he saw Tommy dashing across the West Lawn. Sneaking back after curfew, as usual.

A few minutes later, Tommy quietly entered the room.

Porter heard him breathing hard from his drunken jog across the academy grounds. He had left the lights off, and Tommy hadn't turned them on when he came in. Porter's eyes had adjusted to the dark by then, and he watched as Tommy sat on the edge of his bunk removing his sneakers. "Tommy."

Tommy froze, holding a sneaker in one hand. "That you Porter?"

"Yeah." A pause. "Who else would it be?"

"You never know," Tommy said with a soft laugh. He removed his other sneaker. "Why you sitting here in the dark?"

"Just thinking."

Tommy strode across the room and flicked the lights on. Porter squinted as the light played tricks with his pupils.

"You're making me nervous."

"Thinking makes you nervous?" asked Porter.

"It does when you're the one doing it."

Porter chuckled.

"What's up, man?" Tommy asked again. "You look a mess."

"I had a little accident."

"It's not just that," Tommy said, slipping out of his jeans. He had thighs like tree trunks. "You've got this look like . . . I don't know—like you're losing it. Going wacko."

"You're not helping my paranoia any, big guy. I was just wondering about that myself."

Tommy dropped his jeans over the back of a chair. "Anything I can do to help?"

Porter gave Tommy a weak smile. "Put a bullet in my head if I start to foam at the mouth?" But then he had a second thought. "Let me borrow your car."

"My car? What for?"

"I want to take a little ride into the city," Porter said, fingering the matchbook he still held in his hand.

"Now?" Tommy asked, giving Porter a funny look.

"Yeah. Now."

"Why? What's up?"

Porter tossed Tommy the matchbook. "I want to check this place out."

Tommy looked at the matchbook. "What's the matter? Not enough excitement at the Night Owl for you?"

Porter gave him a little laugh. "Too much, actually."

"But things should start to calm down now, right?"

"What do you mean?" Porter asked.

"I mean someone did us both a favor by knocking off the Jaggers, right? Now you don't have to go to the police, right? There's no way they can kick us out of the academy now, right?"

Porter hadn't the heart to tell him that they were

186

in it deeper than ever. That he was the leading suspect in the murder of the Jaggers. And Tommy, too, by default. Porter remembered what Detective Bronson had said about the possibility of Porter hiring someone to do the killing for him. It wouldn't take much digging to find out that Tommy was Porter's roommate and sometime bodyguard. Then Porter and Tommy could both kiss their scholarships and the academy goodbye.

In fact, Porter could probably kiss his *ass* goodbye if Tommy got kicked out of the academy because of him.

"Ain't that right, Porter?" Tommy asked anxiously. "It should be clear sailing from now until graduation, huh?"

"That's right big guy. Our troubles are over."

"So what's put the bug up your butt?"

Porter smiled wistfully. "Girl trouble, bro. Know what I mean?"

Getting rid of girls was the only girl trouble Tommy ever had. "You trying to dump . . . what's-her-name . . . Jamie? You just met this chick."

"Not quite. I'm trying to hold on to her. She, ah . . . wants to run away and be a topless dancer at the Savage Limbo. I thought maybe I could talk her out of it."

Tommy shook his head sadly as he tossed Porter the car keys. "My Fiat's still parked at the Night Owl." Where he always left it when he couldn't get back in time to beat the curfew.

"Thanks, big guy," Porter said, taking the keys. He slipped on a dark wool sweater and grabbed his wallet.

"Think you can make it over the wall?"

Porter shrugged. "Well, if I can't, I'll be back to tuck you in," he joked.

"Get your fingers broken . . ." was the last thing Porter heard Tommy say as he slipped out the door and down the hall. He made it over the wall, barely, and back to the Night Owl parking lot. He found Tommy's rust bucket Fiat and cranked the motor over and headed for the city. It was about an hour's drive, which gave him another hour to think. Another hour to try and figure out what the hell he was doing.

Whether he liked it or not, weird things were happening to him. If he did nothing, things were *still* going to happen to him. So, he figured, he might as well try to make something happen himself. He had nothing to lose.

Except, of course, his life.

But his life might already be in danger—if Meat Bomb thought Porter was part of the Jaggers' gang. Porter accepted the possibility that he was on a wild goose chase, but he had a feeling Meat Bomb had gone back to the city after the Night Owl had closed. Back to the Savage Limbo. He didn't know if Meat Bomb was looking for him or not—if he wanted to kill him or not. But he wasn't going to spend the rest of his life looking over his shoulder waiting to find out.

A plan started to form in his head.

He was pretty sure Meat Bomb murdered the Jaggers. And if what Booger had told him was true— Booger was next in line. The problem was getting the police to see it that way. Redirect their investigation away from him and onto Meat Bomb. Porter had to gain the biker's confidence, somehow.

He had to get Meat Bomb to confess to the murder of the Jaggers.

Porter drove across the upper level of the George Washington Bridge and into the bright lights of the big city. Even at this late an hour, traffic still flowed in and out of the city that never slept, but at least it wasn't bumper to bumper. He took the Hudson River Drive exit south to 14th Street. Then he went east to First Avenue and then south again to the East Village.

He found the Savage Limbo on a small side street near St. Marks Place. It was hard to miss with the row of Harley-Davidsons parked out front. He had to go around the block twice before finding a parking spot. Then he made his way back to the Savage Limbo.

He stood in front of the entrance trying to work up the nerve to go in. He was about to change his mind when a girl with jet black hair cut punkish style and a safety pin piercing her nose brushed past him. She opened the door to the bar and Porter's nostrils were assailed by a blast of moldy air and warm beer. The girl glanced over her shoulder at Porter. "You coming in or just looking?"

Porter followed her in.

The Savage Limbo was a seedy dive. It made the Night Owl seem like the Taj Mahal in comparison. Porter walked up to the bar with the girl. He thought he might look a little less conspicuous if he were with someone. She didn't seem to mind when he offered to buy her a drink. She ordered a shot of tequila. Porter ordered a beer for himself.

The bartender, a burned out looking character roughly between twenty-five and sixty-five, whose pants defied gravity, didn't even bother to card him. Porter nursed his beer as he looked around, taking the place in. He looked back at the girl, who was staring at him with a whimsical expression on her face. "Nice haircut," she said, knocking back her shot of tequila and sucking on a wedge of lime. She smacked her lips with satisfaction. "I hear whitewalls are in this year."

"Thanks," Porter said. "I like that thing in your nose."

"Really?" she asked, fingering the pin. "It's pure copper."

"No kidding," Porter said, eyeing her empty shot glass.

"Another?"

"Thanks."

Porter held up his finger to the bartender and pointed to the girl's shot glass. The bartender poured the girl another and silently took the money from a small pile of bills that Porter had left on the bar in front of him. The bartender ambled down to the other end of the bar with his butt cheeks on display and the girl sprinkled salt on her hand before downing the shot and doing the sucking bit again. Porter took a sip of his beer. He thought he might be getting a contact high from all the pot smoke in the place.

"What's your name?" he asked the girl.

"Tempest," she said.

Porter grinned. "Nice name. Very Shakespearean. Is that your *real* name."

"What's it to you?" she shot back hostilely.

"Uh, nothing, really," Porter said, amicably. She didn't look like the type of girl he wanted to argue with. She didn't ask him what his name was, and he didn't volunteer it. "Do you know a guy named Meat Bomb?"

"Yeah, I know Meat," she said, pulling a home-made cigarette from the pocket of her fake zebra jacket. "You're a cop, aren't you?"

Porter pointed to himself. "Me? A cop? Do I look like a cop?"

"Yeah. Right out of the academy," Tempest said.

Porter scanned the bar. It looked like a meeting hall for aging bikers. There were a bunch of them around a pool table displaying their colors on the backs of their black leather jackets.

The Holy Savages.

"You got a match?" Tempest asked.

"Yeah, sure," Porter said, digging into his jacket pocket for the matchbook that Meat Bomb had left at the Night Owl. He lit her cigarette.

"What do you want Meat for?" she asked, blowing a stream of pungent smoke in Porter's direction.

"I, ah . . ." Porter shrugged as he waved the smoke away. "Wanted to return his matches?"

Tempest gave Porter a sour look. "You're kind of a smartass, you know that?"

Porter grinned. "That's what they tell me."

Tempest swiveled on her stool. "Yo, Meat!" Porter felt a ripple of fear shimmy up his spine. Tempest put her fingers to her lips and whistled shrilly. "Meat!"

Porter sat rigid on his bar stool as a shadow fell

across the bar top in front of him. "Meat," Tempest said. "Junior here was looking for ya."

Porter looked up and saw Meat Bomb reflected in the dingy bar mirror. He must have weighed at least three hundred pounds, Porter estimated.

"You looking for me?"

Porter slowly turned on his stool and looked Meat Bomb in the eye, putting on a show of bravado he didn't feel. "Remember me? Meat Bomb bristled, and Porter prepared to have his bones snapped. "I was at the Night Owl the other night when you were there."

"Who says I was there?"

"I saw you," Porter said.

"How'd you know it was me? How'd you find me here?"

"A friend of mine says he knows you."

Meat Bomb leaned in closer to Porter, resting a massive forearm on the bar railing. "Were these friends . . . the Jaggers?"

"You got to be kidding," Porter snorted. "The Jaggers were the two biggest scumbags I ever met. They were trying to horn in on my action. In fact, I was thinking of getting rid of them until someone beat me to it. I'd like to meet the guy who did it someday and thank him personally. He did us all a favor."

Meat Bomb allowed Porter a smile. "Okay, let's cut the crap. Whatta you want from me?"

Porter's mind was whirring, he was improvising his story as he went. "I, ah . . . go the Hudson Military Academy, in Cooper Hollow, and I thought you might be interested in going into business with me."

"What kind of business?"

"I'm looking for a supplier. And believe me, I got plenty of clients at the academy. It's an all boys school. And most of the guys who go there have parents with money growing on trees. I'd even cut you in for a percentage of the action."

Meat Bomb seemed to be mulling it over. "Who was this friend of yours who told you about me. What was his name?"

Porter swallowed hard. "Freddy Burger. Only everyone calls him Booger."

A strange light shone in Meat Bomb's eyes. "I'd like to meet this friend of yours before I do any business."

"Sure," Porter said confidently.

"Tomorrow night. At the Night Owl."

"No problem."

"But don't tell him I'm coming, all right? I want it to be a surprise," Meat Bomb said with a malicious grin.

"However you want to do it, Mr. Barker. Or should I call you Meat?"

Barker ignored Porter's question. "Tomorrow night at the Night Owl. Eight o'clock." Then he turned and walked away.

Well, Porter thought, that wasn't too hard.

Now if he could only think of what to do next.

He got up to leave. He even left the bartender a tip.

"Hey?" Tempest called after him.

Porter turned around.

"You going to drink your beer?"

Porter smiled. "Go for it."

"Thanks sweetie," she said, reaching for the beer mug. She held it up as if to toast him. "It was nice knowing you."

Tommy's red Fiat wasn't exactly made for sleeping in, as Porter found out that night in the Night Owl parking lot. He wondered how Tommy could even squeeze his big frame into the tiny car. Porter spent what was left of the night scrunched up in the back-seat listening to the car heater rattle as he tried to nod off for a few hours.

Or maybe it was his own frenzied thoughts he was listening to, rattling around inside his head like a pair of dice, as he tried to come up with a plan to save his skinny ass. He had slept in the car to avoid getting caught climbing back over the wall. He had only a few more hours until his next class anyway.

By dawn he had come up with a plan.

Tomorrow—today—he'd cut class and say he had a doctor's appointment off campus.

First, he'd have a little talk with Detective Bronson. He would tell him that he had done some investigating on his own and he thought he knew who had killed the Jaggers. In fact, the suspect would be at the Night Owl Club that night to make a bogus drug deal with Porter. All Bronson had to do was wire him. They'd talk business for a while and then Porter would work the conversation around to the Jaggers' murder. Then all he had to do was get Meat Bomb to admit to doing it.

It sounded simple enough.

Porter dragged himself into the Cooper Hollow Police Station and asked the cop at the front desk for Detective Bronson. The desk sergeant picked up the phone and punched in an extension number. He said a few words into the phone before directing Porter to Bronson's office. Porter walked down a dingy gray corridor through a chorus of ringing phones and clattering typewriters.

After finding Bronson in his office fiddling with a fishing rod, Porter began to lay out his plan to him.

Bronson set aside his fishing pole, leaned back in his squeaky swivel chair, and stuck his size thirteen brogans up on the desk top. "Look kid," he said, taking a sip from a cardboard cup of coffee. "If you have some solid evidence pertaining to this case, let's hear it, all right? I'm a busy man. I don't have time for this nonsense."

Busy with what? Porter wondered. Keeping his swivel chair warm? Dreaming up new fishing spots? Thinking about his retirement plans? *"I* don't *have* the evidence. *I* want *you* to wire *me* so *we* can *get* the evidence," Porter said, spelling it out for the detective slowly and clearly.

Bronson shot Porter a nasty look. "Now just who is this suspect?"

"Meat—I mean, Sonny Barker. He runs a biker club on the Lower East Side of Manhattan. A gang called the Holy Savages." Even in Bronson's thick skull, Porter could hear a bell ringing.

"Sonny Barker, eh?" Bronson said.

"Yeah."

"Sonny Barker's on Rikers Island awaiting trial on a drug charge," Bronson said, as if that fact totally destroyed Porter's credibility.

"Well, he must have a good lawyer because he's out now. I'm meeting him tonight at the Night Owl."

"Now let me get this straight," Bronson said with a smirk, crossing his arms over his chest. "You're meeting Barker tonight at the Night Owl, and he's going to confess to you that he murdered the Jaggers?"

"Well . . . yeah, something like that. I think I can get him to talk about it. All you have to do is wire me. We can get it all down on tape. And, I don't know, maybe set up a video camera somewhere to film—"

"Whoa, whoa," Bronson said with a laugh. "You've been watching too many cop shows, kid. This is the Cooper Hollow Police Department—we're not the FBI. We don't have the manpower or the equipment for an extensive stake out—"

"It's not an *extensive* stake out," Porter snapped angrily, losing his patience. "One night is all I'm asking for. If you don't have the resources then borrow them from the FBI or a neighboring district or something . . ." Bronson had picked up his fishing pole and was fiddling with it again. "What's your problem, man?" Porter wanted to take that damn pole and stick it up Bronson's nose.

Bronson looked up sharply at Porter. "Watch your tone of voice with me, sonny boy," Bronson snapped back. "I thought they taught you cadets at the academy to respect authority."

Porter fought to control his temper. "One night.

That's all I'm asking for. Wire me up and listen in, that's all you have to do. I'm taking all the risks." Bronson was untangling his fishing line. "You won't be in any danger if that's what you're worried about."

Bronson turned red in the face. "Now look, you little snotnose," he said angrily. "If you have any hard evidence, then produce it." He yanked open his desk drawer and pulled out an envelope, tossed it to Porter. "Like this."

Porter opened the envelope and looked at a familiar set of pictures. The photos of him in the front seat of the Jaggers' car.

"I found those in the glove compartment of Skip Jagger's car. You wanna tell me what that's all about? Or are you sticking with your story that you don't know the Jaggers?"

Porter gave up and walked out of the cop's office. Obviously Bronson had already pigeon-holed him as another worthless punk like the Jaggers. *Who needs him anyway,* Porter thought. *I'll do it myself.*

He still had Tommy's tape recorder.

Wednesday night

Porter sat nervously in his booth at the Night Owl and waited for Meat Bomb to arrive. He patted Tommy's tape recorder, which he had clipped to his belt beneath his jacket. He left the middle buttons on his jacket undone so he could slip his hand inside to turn the recorder on.

Maybe he should do it now, he thought. Except that Meat Bomb was already late, and he didn't know how much later he would be. If he turned it on now, he would probably get an hour of his pounding heart or his churning stomach. Porter took a deep breath and tried to fight back the fear that gripped his chest like a giant vise.

He was feeling terribly alone.

He hadn't seen Jamie anywhere. Did she really believe he had anything to do with the Jaggers' murder? Probably not. But she knew he had lied to her, and she was pretty mad about that, and the scene he had made in the Night Owl. Well, if his plan worked, maybe he could get her back. *If* it worked.

He hadn't seen Booger anywhere, either.

He was counting on Booger being here tonight. He wanted him sitting in the booth with him when Meat Bomb arrived. He knew Booger wouldn't be too crazy about the idea at first, and he couldn't blame him, but Porter was confident he'd go along with it once he realized what his plan was.

Porter knew that Meat Bomb wasn't coming to the Night Owl to discuss drugs. He was coming for Booger. Booger had helped murder his brother, and Meat Bomb wanted revenge. But would he be satisfied with only Booger? Or would he try to kill Porter as well? Meat Bomb wouldn't want any witnesses.

Porter needed Booger for bait. And Booger *had* agreed to help. He needed Booger to steer the conversation away from dealing drugs and to the Jaggers' murder. He thought the best way to do that would be to talk about the murder of the younger Barker. It didn't matter how he did it. Booger could deny any involvement in the murder or admit to doing it and beg for Meat Bomb's forgiveness. It didn't matter which, really. Meat Bomb would forgive him all right, as he was splintering every bone in his body, but that wasn't the point. He had to get Meat Bomb to talk about the murder of the Jaggers. He had to get him to admit to doing it.

Porter was counting on Meat Bomb not trying anything violent inside the Night Owl. At least not right out in the open. He would probably make up some bogus story about having the dope in his car or something like that and then when they went out to get it . . .

Porter heard some gasps from the front of the room and looked up in time to see Meat Bomb walk into the club.

Porter's limbs tingled with nervous energy.

Meat Bomb looked around, saw Porter, walked over. "Where's your pal?" Meat Bomb asked, looking down at Porter.

Porter glanced at his watch. "He should be here any minute, Meat. Pull up a chair." He sure as hell wasn't going to fit in the booth seat, Porter knew. Meat Bomb pulled a chair over from the next table.

Porter took the opportunity to quickly flick the recorder on with a trembling hand. Meat Bomb sat down in the chair and leaned on the booth table. The table made a creaking sound but held up. He and Porter were face to face, but neither spoke.

Porter heard some moaning and a rustling sound come from somewhere near his midsection. It sounded like a couple making love. Then Porter heard Tommy's voice; a girl's voice responded with a giggle.

Porter had pushed the play button by mistake.

"What the hell . . ." Meat Bomb said. He reached over and yanked Porter's jacket open, popping several buttons, and pulled out the recorder. "You little son of a bitch," he muttered, crushing the little Sony in one hand.

Before Porter could get out of the booth and make a run for it, Meat Bomb slid off his chair and sat on the edge of the booth seat—as much as he could get his massive butt on—effectively blocking Porter's escape. He slipped a big beefy arm around Porter's shoulder in what looked like a friendly gesture. Then Porter felt his meaty fingers gently slip around his throat.

He wouldn't kill me right here, would he? In a crowded night club? In front of everyone?

Porter could hear the heavy wheezing of his breath, and feel his fingers tightening around his neck.

Yes, he would.

Porter squirmed in his seat. He opened his mouth to yell, but Meat Bomb tightened his grip around Porter's throat. Now Porter knew what it felt like to be a mouse trapped beneath a cat's paw. The pressure on his jugular increased.

My god, he's going to kill me right here in the booth.

The room began to swirl like stars in the Milky Way as Meat Bomb's fingers slowly and gently crushed the life out of him. Porter felt himself slipping into the final darkness.

"Excuse me, sir," Porter vaguely heard the waitress' voice coming from what seemed a million miles away. "Did you order a pitcher of ginger ale?" That was odd; the Night Owl didn't have waitresses. Then he felt a cool splash as the room shot back into focus. He saw Jamie standing there. Meat Bomb had been splashed with most of the soda. He was soaked in it, his beard plastered back in sudsy liquid.

A hush fell over the room as every eye in the room turned in the direction of their table.

Porter slipped his left arm out and brought his elbow back down hard on the tip of Meat Bomb's nose, a karate move Tommy had taught him. Tommy had always stressed that no matter how big or strong your opponent was, the bones in the nose weren't any bigger or stronger than the average person's. The blow would hurt like hell and make the eyes water like crazy, temporarily blinding your assailant.

Good ol' Tommy. Porter had actually learned something from him after all.

Porter felt soft cartilage snap beneath the impact of the blow. Meat Bomb's nose burst open like a broken ketchup bottle. He loosened his grip on Porter's throat. Porter clamored over the top of the table and leapt to the floor. He was running before his feet even touched the ground. Meat Bomb made a grab for him and caught the end of his denim jacket, pulling Porter back even as blood continued to flow from his broken nose. Porter stomped down as hard as he could on Meat Bomb's instep. His thick motorcycle boot absorbed most of the shock, but it was enough to distract him. Porter slipped out of his jacket and bolted from the room.

Like an angry bear, the biker rose to his feet with a roar. He tipped the booth table like it was made of cardboard and sent it crashing to the floor. Meat Bomb chased after Porter with surprising speed for a man his size, scattering the patrons of the club like bowling pins. He ran through the arched doorway into the adjoining room, stopping at the base of the stairs that led to the upper floor.

"Where'd that punk run to?" Meat Bomb bellowed to a tall, thin man with a shock of white hair and an apron tied around his waist.

"Maybe you'd better calm down fella—"

Meat Bomb grabbed Jake Demos and effortlessly lifted him into the air. "Look, you old coot, I'm in no mood to argue. Now which way did he go!"

Jake's reply was to point up the stairs.

Meat Bomb dropped Jake and clomped up the stairs. He looked down a long hallway. At the end of the hallway was a closed door. The door slowly creaked open.

The punk must be hiding in there, Meat Bomb suspected. He ran down the hallway. The kid must've come this way. There was no other way he could have gone.

Meat Bomb reached the end of the hallway and yanked open the door. He was greeted with a wash of cool air and a funky smell he was at a loss to identify. He entered the room and looked around.

The door suddenly slammed shut behind him.

Meat Bomb was enveloped in a sea of darkness. Startled, he tried to pry open the closed door. But even his great strength couldn't budge it. He heard a rustling in the darkness and turned to face the noise. Then he heard something like chains being dragged across a wooden floor. In the dim light he saw something come at him. Something with red, luminous eyes.

His scream was long and agonizing.

They could hear it all the way to the first floor.

It was freezing in the woods without his jacket.

But Porter didn't care. He knew he could always buy another jacket, but he had only one life. He ran down the trail through the damp woods until he had no more breath to fuel him. Feeling safe, he slowed down, but kept to a steady pace, just in case. He didn't think a man as big as Meat Bomb could catch him in the open woods. Even if he knew which trail he had taken. Thank God for Jamie. She had saved him, again.

He thought he heard a noise on the trail behind him.

He stopped and listened.

Someone was running toward him.

Porter picked up his pace, but his pursuer was still gaining on him. In desperation, Porter hid behind a clump of bushes. He sucked up air in greedy gasps and listened for the footsteps.

But all was quiet.

Probably just an animal. Maybe a night owl. The forest sheltered many forms of life. Not all of them were dangerous.

Not all of them.

Porter came out from behind the bush and started to make his way up the trail again. He heard the footsteps coming again, faster than ever, crashing through the woods. He tried to get off the trail, but he caught his foot in a tangle of vines and went sprawling to the ground. His glasses flew from his face and landed in the darkness somewhere in front of him. He scrambled about on his knees, desperately running his hands through the loose leaves, searching for them.

The footsteps grew louder, closer.

Porter couldn't find his glasses. He looked up, but couldn't see very well. All he could see was a dark figure in the moonlight walking his way. He couldn't make out who it was.

The figure approached Porter, also breathing hard.

When he was almost upon Porter, Porter saw that he held a gun in his hand.

Twenty-five

Porter remained perfectly still. As if awaiting the fall of a guillotine blade. Fear was hammering through his system. The dark figure standing over him stepped past him and bent low. He retrieved Porter's glasses from the leaves and handed them to him. After putting them on, he looked up at Porter, silhouetted in the moonlight.

"Is your name Porter Smith?" the man asked. He was wearing some kind of uniform. It took a moment for Porter's senses to straighten themselves out. It was a police uniform.

"Yes, sir," Porter said. The man reached his hand down to help Porter up. Porter took it and pulled himself off the ground.

"My name's Sam Murphy," said the man. "Cooper Hollow Police. My niece asked me to keep an eye on you. Sorry I didn't get to the Night Owl a little earlier. I heard you had a little trouble back there."

"Yes, sir," Porter said, wiping off some dead leaves. "Only he wasn't so little."

"When I got to the Night Owl, Jamie told me you

had been in a fight. She thought you had run out of the club. I ran outside in time to see someone running into the woods. I didn't know if it was you or someone chasing you," Sam said, holstering his gun.

Porter gave him a little laugh. "You nearly scared me to death." He shivered. Officer Sam Murphy was younger than Porter had imagined Jamie's uncle would be. He didn't look to be much older than himself, as a matter of fact. He was a good-looking, dark-haired man, sturdily built, with an open, friendly face.

Sam started to unzip his jacket. "You look cold. Here, take my jacket."

"No thank you, sir," Porter said, rubbing his hands briskly together to generate some heat. "I'm not far from the academy."

Steam billowed from their mouths as they spoke.

"My niece told me you've gotten yourself into a jam. I also heard back at the station that you're a suspect in the Jagger murder case. You want to talk about it?"

"I didn't kill the Jaggers, sir. I think the guy who did it is a biker named Meat Bomb Barker—that's the guy I had the fight with back at the Night Owl. I had this plan to get him to confess to the murder. Only I screwed up, and he found my tape recorder. If Jamie hadn't distracted him, I think he would have killed me right there in the Night Owl. When I heard someone coming after me on the trail, I thought it was him."

"Where is this Barker?"

"The last time I saw him he was still back at the Night Owl."

"What makes you think Barker killed the Jaggers?"

"The Jaggers killed his brother. I know someone who saw the whole thing." Porter decided not to tell him that Booger had actually helped kill the biker's brother.

"Will your witness come forward with this information?"

"I think so," Porter said with more confidence than he felt.

"Then I suggest you try like hell to get him to talk and get back to me before you get yourself into any worse trouble."

"Yes, sir."

"Do it tonight. Find your witness and get back to me. Call the station, and they'll put you through right away. You got that?"

"Yes, sir."

"Don't just keep saying 'yes' if you don't mean it."

"Yes, sir."

"And stop calling me 'sir.' My name's Sam."

"Okay . . . Sam."

"In the meantime, I'm going to go back to the Night Owl and see if I can find this Barker character." He turned to leave, then paused for a moment. "My niece really cares about you, Porter. I don't want to see you get hurt, and I especially don't want to see her get hurt. I want you to give that some serious thought. It's time you got your act together."

"Yes, sir."

Sam grinned and shook his head. "Later," he said over his shoulder as he headed toward the Night Owl.

Porter hurried back to the academy. The cold was digging into him like a frosty knife. Things had gone far enough. Too far, in fact. He no longer cared about making money, or the academy, or college, or Wall Street. He had a girl he cared about, who cared about him. That was the important thing. He decided to play it straight from that moment on and let whatever had to happen, happen.

It was time to stop running.

Now all he had to do was tell Tommy that.

Porter found Tommy back at the room. He had just showered after a late practice and was going over his playbook. The academy had a big game coming up that week against their crosstown rivals, the Cooper Hollow High Red Devils.

Porter told Tommy all about what happened at the Night Owl. And that he intended to find Booger and go to the police. He was going to come clean with everything.

"Did you tell that cop I was involved?"

"No way, man. I'm taking full responsibility, Tommy. I'm going to make it very clear to the cops and Colonel Green that it was all my fault."

"Thanks, pal," Tommy said bitterly. "But do you really think that's going to make a difference?"

No, I don't, Porter thought, but I'm not going to tell him that. Because it would be just another lie, and Porter was through lying. Instead he removed his glasses, and set them on the dresser and waited for Tommy to explode and beat him to a bloody pulp. He wouldn't have lifted a finger to stop him, either.

But Tommy didn't make a move against him.

"You've gone off your rocker, Porter," Tommy finally said in dismay.

"I know it must look that way, big guy."

Tommy breathed out heavily as he walked across the room. He stared out their bedroom window at the academy. Porter could see in his roommate's eyes how much he loved what he saw.

Tommy shrugged. "Well, you know what they say. You gotta be kind to a crazy person or you'll go crazy yourself someday. There's absolutely no way you'll change your mind?"

Porter shook his head sadly. "None."

"Then let's go find Booger," Tommy said, getting dressed.

"You're going to help me?" Porter asked, surprised.

"That's right, little buddy."

Porter glanced at his watch. "We might not make it back before curfew."

Tommy gave Porter a bemused look. "Curfew?" He laughed. "After tonight we're not going to have to worry about curfew anymore, Porter."

Porter looked at Tommy with a sinking feeling. He had resigned himself to his fate, but for Tommy, the reality had to be a bit more jolting. Tommy loved the academy and all that it stood for. Getting kicked out had to be like losing a close member of his family. He had to be going out of his mind inside, and yet he took it like a man—more than that—he was even willing to help him find Booger and clear his name. Tommy was a true friend in every sense of the word.

Tommy finished dressing. He grabbed his jacket

and patted the pockets to make sure his wallet and keys were still there. He looked at Porter. "Let's do it, man," he said, slipping out the door. Porter grabbed a heavy sweater and hurried after him.

They drove back to the Night Owl in silence. Porter tried to think of something to say, but every time he looked at Tommy, his face was fixed with that don't-bug-me-now expression Porter knew so well.

They drove into the Night Owl parking lot.

Tommy looked over at Porter. "You know, you might be safer here in the car, in case that Barker creep's still in there. Why don't you let me go in and take a look. See if Booger's there. Or if he isn't, I can ask around a little, maybe find out where he lives."

Porter nodded.

Tommy wasn't gone long. He came back without Booger and jumped into the Fiat, cranked over the ignition. "Booger wasn't there. He heard Meat Bomb was on the prowl and went into hiding. But he left word with Jenny Demos where we could find him."

"Where?"

"At the cemetery."

"Where?" Porter thought he had heard incorrectly.

"Riverside Cemetery."

"Why would he go there?" Porter asked, incredulous.

Tommy shrugged. "Maybe he figured that's the last place Meat Bomb would look for him."

They arrived at Riverside Cemetery, one of the oldest in Cooper Hollow, and got out of the car. They walked up to the wrought-iron gate that served as an entrance.

"Where are we suppose to meet him?" Porter asked.

"Down by the river," Tommy said, stopping at the entrance.

Dark clouds roiled in the moonlight. Tommy looked up into the agitated sky, then back at Porter. "Looks like rain, lemme check the trunk of my car to see if I have an umbrella in there. You go on ahead and see if you can find Booger before he gets cold feet and splits. I'll meet you down by the river if you can't find him."

Porter nodded and went on ahead, past the rich section of the graveyard with its ornate monuments and fancy mausoleums, past the Oswald Cooper Monument, past history and tradition, down to the river, to Potter's Field. This was the section of the cemetery where the John and Jane Does were buried, or the disenfranchised, those with a name but no money, ended up.

Porter stood by the river edge for a moment and watched its waters run by him, dark and churning. He looked back at the graveyard as a flash of lightning illuminated the jagged tombstones that jutted out of the ground like rows of rotten teeth.

"Booger!" he called.

No answer.

He thought he heard a rustling sound down by the river bank. He looked around. A fog was drifting in. Porter hoped Tommy would hurry up—this place was definitely giving him the creeps. He heard soft, squishing footsteps in the damp ground come his way. He braced himself. The eerie atmosphere had him spooked good, and he was relieved to see Tommy walk toward him carrying a large canvas bag and a flashlight.

"I don't see Booger anywhere. Do you think it's all a big goof?"

"No," Tommy said, shining the light around.

"I'll kill him if it is," Porter said, jamming his frigid hands into his jeans pockets.

"I'm sure he's here," Tommy said confidently.

A jagged bolt of lightning sliced through the sky, followed by a loud boom of thunder, making Porter jump. "Jesus," he said, shaken up. "Couldn't he have just met us at the Bowl-A-Rama or something?"

"I don't think so," Tommy said, shining the flashlight on a row of tombstones. He apparently found what he was looking for. He carried the canvas bag over to a freshly filled grave and sat it down, took out a pick and shovel.

Porter looked on curiously. "Whatta you got there, big guy?"

Tommy jammed the pick in the ground, picked up the shovel. "I'm glad I held on to these. I was going to use them the other night in the woods, to bury Booger. Before the Jaggers came up with that bright idea of breaking into the Night Owl and hanging him in that room with the . . . what did you call it?"

Porter stared at Tommy in confused silence.

Tommy snapped his fingers. "Oh yeah, the pentacle."

"What's going on, Tommy?" Porter asked.

A bolt of lightning flashed across the sky, colossal and jagged, lighting up Tommy's face. Porter had

212

known Tommy for a long time, but he had never seen him look quite like this before. Instead of his usual dumb grin, his lips were pressed together into a cruel, straight line.

"What's going on, big guy?" Porter asked again, fear tingeing his voice this time.

"You were set up, Porter. From the beginning. It wasn't an accident that the Jaggers knew about your gambling operation. I told them about it."

"Huh?"

"You weren't the only one I was placing bets with. I had some action going with the Jaggers, too." Tommy shrugged self-consciously. "I didn't mean to deprive you of business, bud, but you only took those penny-ante bets. I needed some heavier action."

A greater high, Porter thought. He hadn't realized that Tommy's addiction to gambling had taken that turn.

"Only the Jaggers weren't so forgiving when I was late paying them back, the way you were. They held quite a few markers on me and threatened to turn them over to Colonel Green if I didn't do what they said. You see, they were blackmailing me, too."

Porter just shook his head.

"When I found you hog-tied behind the firing range, that wasn't an accident, Porter. And obviously, the Jaggers didn't care if you used me as a bodyguard because they knew all along that I was really working for them. The warning in the shower, that was me. The note in the room, I left that, not Booger. Remember when I told you I went to check to see if the guard had caught him going over the wall? I went to use the phone. I called the Jaggers to tip them off.

Booger knew too much about the Jaggers. That's why he was running, he knew the Jaggers would never just let him go like that. I don't know if he knew I was working for them too, but if he did, and he squealed, I'd go down with them. I couldn't take that chance."

"So . . . you killed them?"

Tommy nodded.

"Dude . . . I would've paid off your markers if it was that bad."

Tommy took a deep breath, looked down at the ground. "Well, as you probably know by now, things have a way of getting out of hand. The Jaggers had a ton of money riding on that big game we have against Cooper Hollow this weekend. They felt pretty confident of winning, too, since they had me in the game shaving points."

Porter shook his head sadly. "How could you, man? You love the academy and the team too much to ever do that."

"You just answered you own question, little buddy. I couldn't do it. And that's what I told them." He shook his head sadly. "But those Jaggers . . . they just won't take no for an answer. You know that."

"I still can't believe you would murder someone."

Tommy reached into his pocket, pulled out Skip's ivory dice and rolled them to Porter's feet, where they came up snake eyes. "Believe it, little buddy."

The sky came alive with persistent flashes of lightning. The first few drops of rain began to fall. Porter stared at Tommy, openmouthed. "And now you're going to kill me?"

Tommy gave Porter a sad look. "Porter . . . I'm

214

doing you a favor. You're only going to end up in a padded cell somewhere."

"What are you talking about?" Porter couldn't believe his oldest friend was actually going to murder him. It had to be some kind of stupid joke to pay back Porter for his mean remarks all these years. He studied Tommy's face, waiting for him to break out in that stupid grin of his, signaling that the charade was over. But Tommy's expression wasn't changing.

"You've totally lost it, Porter. You're crazy. Certifiably insane. The guys with straight-jackets are coming for you, little buddy. All this crap about Booger still being alive. You've gone completely out of your mind—"

"He is alive!" Porter shrieked. "We're meeting him. Here. Tonight. Did you forget, you big blockhead? That's why we're here!"

The air became unusually quiet as Tommy just stared at Porter. "Dude, Booger's *dead.* The Jaggers murdered him in the woods that night. I was there, I saw it. Remember, I was supposed to go with you, but I told you I pulled extra guard duty. It was all part of the scam. I didn't have extra duty. I was in the woods that night. Hiding from *you.* I was the lookout. We were waiting for you, man."

"Booger's . . . dead?" Porter looked into Tommy's face with incomprehension. "And you knew they were going to kill him?"

"I cut him down from the tree. I carried him into the Night Owl. I strung him up in that room. I was *in* there when you came in. Waiting for the Jaggers. The plan was to scare you into keeping your mouth shut so they could keep making money off you."

215

Tommy gave Porter a malicious grin. "But I had plans of my own."

"Booger's dead? Get out of here! I saw him. At the Night Owl . . ." Porter felt sick.

"If you did, then you were the only one," Tommy said, shining the flashlight on the tombstone he was standing next to. Porter stared at the tombstone, his eyes wide, at the inscription illuminated by the beam of light.

Freddy Burger. R.I.P.

"Like I said, man, you're nuts," Tommy said, shining the flashlight in Porter's face.

The rain fell harder.

Porter stared down at the freshly dug grave. "No way, man. I know he's not down in there."

"I thought it would be kind of cute if you joined your pal. You two were an awful lot alike, you know. He reminded me a lot of you when we went to St. Ignatius together. Don't you think that's a good idea, Porter. You know, just dig a deeper hole and stuff you down in there with him, then cover you both up real nice and throw the extra dirt into the river. No one would ever know what happened to you. Don't you think that's a smart idea, Porter?" Tommy asked bitterly. Tommy's laugh was harsh. "Who would think of looking for a missing body in a graveyard? I think that's pretty damn smart of me. Don't you, Porter?"

But Porter didn't answer. He sprinted away from Tommy, but his foot caught on an exposed tree root, and he fell just a few feet away, savagely twisting his ankle.

Tommy looked down at him lying there pathetically on the ground. He had a shining, demented gaze as he walked toward him. "You always thought I was so stupid, didn't you Porter? For years you thought that. You're such a smug little wiseass. But maybe *you're* the stupid one, little buddy—" He raised the shovel to bring it crashing down on Porter's head.

"Hey stupid!" came a voice out of the fog.

Tommy looked up and the breath hissed out of him in a sharp gasp.

"That grave's not big enough for the two of us."

"Oh my god, no," Tommy cried, dropping the shovel.

A dark figure walked out of the fog, rain pelting off his Devil's cap. Porter looked over his shoulder and recoiled in horror when he saw that it was Booger.

Tommy slowly backed away, his face twisted in a grimace of terror and revulsion.

"I suppose I should thank you for hanging me up in the Room of the Dead," Booger said. "You gave me new life. Although I'm not sure if it's exactly what I had in mind when I died. I thought I'd be dead, not undead."

The wind tore into the sky above them.

"You should've just killed Porter and dumped his body into the river instead of bringing him here. Instead of being a wiseass. Instead of violating my home. Like you did to my friends in the Room of the Dead. That's trespassing, pal. That's really stupid."

"No!" Tommy shrieked as a jagged bolt of lightning lanced earthward over Porter's head and struck

217

the ground in front of him. The blast threw his body up into the air.

When the smoke had cleared, Porter rose shakily to his feet. He saw Tommy next to Booger's grave lying on his back in a twisted heap. The sharp end of the pick had slammed through his back, piercing his heart, before puncturing the chest wall.

Booger walked over to Porter, who was shivering, his body soaked from the freezing wet rain. He took off his Red Devils jacket and gave it to Porter, who took it, too dazed to say anything. "You look like you could use this."

Then he removed his Red Devils cap, displaying a clean round hole in his forehead. "And this."

Porter could plainly see the path Skip Jagger's bullet had taken as it punched a hole through Booger's skull.

"I won't be needing them anymore," Booger said, with a trace of sadness in his voice.

Porter looked at Booger and thought his mind might come unhinged. "Y-you said you were alive. Back at the Night Owl. S-sitting in the booth."

Booger grinned. "If I told you I was dead, you would have been halfway to China by now. I made a deal with . . . my friends . . . in the Room of the Dead. I was doomed to drift through limbo with them for all eternity unless I prevented the same fate from happening to you. Unless I stopped your murder. Back at the Greyhound station, when you gave me all your money, I told you that I owed you one. I couldn't rest in peace until I paid back that debt." Booger smiled wanly. "Now we're even."

Porter began to shake uncontrollably, and it wasn't

from the cold. He watched speechlessly as Booger's body seemed to vaporize and become one with the fog that surrounded him.

It was the last time he—or anyone—would ever see Booger again.

Epilogue

Porter didn't wait to get kicked out of the academy. He resigned before going to the police.

He told the police his story. All of it. As he expected and as Tommy predicted—maybe he really wasn't that stupid after all—they thought he was crazy. He spent the rest of the year undergoing court ordered psychiatric evaluation.

But he stuck to his story.

He was through lying.

The hospital released him in time for him to take his senior year over again at Cooper Hollow High. He wore Booger's Red Devil's jacket and cap to school every day, regardless of the weather.

Jamie and he became an item, and they made plans to go to college together. Jamie didn't care what anyone thought of Porter, she was a little crazy herself and wasn't shy about admitting it. They were two peas in a pod. Or maybe two nuts in the same shell would have been more accurate. Either way, they were made for each other.

As Jenny Demos knew the first time she saw them both in the Night Owl Club.

YOU WON'T BE SCARED . . . *NOT*
AND YOU'LL *SCREAM* FOR MORE!
Bone-chilling horror from Z-FAVE

SCREAM #1: BLOOD PACT   (4355, $3.50)
Jamie Fox and her friends decide to fake a "suicide" pact
when they find out their hang out, an old train depot, is going to be demolished. They sign their names in blood, but of
course, never really intend to kill themselves.

Now, one by one, the signers of the pact begin to die in
what looks like suicide. But Jamie suspects murder, and will
be the next to die . . . unless she can unmask the cunning
killer who's watching her every move!

SCREAM #2: DEADLY DELIVERY   (4356, $3.50)
Derek Cliver and his friends have recently joined The Terror
Club, an exciting new mail-order club, which allows them
the fantasy of "disposing" of those that they despise with
monsters of their own creation. But now the game is terrify-
ingly real because these monsters have come to life—and are
actually killing.

The body count is rising as Derek and his friends somehow must undo what they've done . . . before they become
the next victims!

SCREAM #3: WANTED TO RENT   (4357, $3.50)
Sixteen-year-old Christy Baker is really worried. There is
something about her family's handsome boarder that gives
her the creeps. Things get even creepier when she finds a
length of rope, masking tape, newspaper clippings about
murdered women . . . and a photo of herself . . . in his
room.

Now Christy is home alone. The downstairs door has just
opened. She knows who's come in—and why he's there!

*Available wherever paperbacks are sold, or order direct from the
Publisher. Send cover price plus 50¢ per copy for mailing and handling to Zebra Books, Dept. 4450, 475 Park Avenue South, New
York, N.Y. 10016. Residents of New York and Tennessee must include sales tax. DO NOT SEND CASH. For a free Zebra/Pinnacle
catalog please write to the above address.*

HAUTALA'S HORROR—HOLD ON
TO YOUR HEAD!

**WHEN YOU HAVE GIRL FRIENDS —
YOU HAVE IT ALL!**

Follow the trials, triumph, and awesome adventures of five special girls that have become fast friends in spite of — or because of their differences!

Janis Sandifer-Wayne,	a peace-loving, vegetarian veteran of protests and causes.
Stephanie Ling,	the hard-working oldest daughter of a single parent.
Natalie Bell,	Los Angeles refugee and street-smart child of an inter-racial marriage.
Cassandra Taylor,	Natalie's cousin and the sophisticated daughter of an upper-middle class African-American family.
Maria Torres,	a beautiful cheerleader who's the apple of her conservative parent's eye.

They're all juniors at Seven Pines High. And they're doing things their own way — together!

GIRLFRIENDS #1: DRAW THE LINE   (4350, $3.50)
by Nicole Grey

GIRLFRIENDS #2: DO THE RIGHT THING   (4351, $3.50)
by Nicole Grey

GIRLFRIENDS #3: DEAL ME OUT   (4352, $3.50)
by Nicole Grey